D0551668

A CROWN FOR THE KING

Solomon ibn Gabirol

A CROWN FOR THE KING

Translated by
David R. Slavitt

New York   Oxford

Oxford University Press

1998

Oxford University Press

Oxford   New York

Athens   Auckland   Bangkok   Bogotá   Buenos Aires   Calcutta
Cape Town   Chennai   Dar es Salaam   Delhi   Florence   Hong Kong   Istanbul
Karachi   Kuala Lumpur   Madrid   Melbourne   Mexico City   Mumbai
Nairobi   Paris   São Paulo   Singapore   Taipei   Tokyo   Toronto   Warsaw

and associated companies in
Berlin   Ibadan

Copyright © 1998 by David R. Slavitt

Published by Oxford University Press, Inc.
198 Madison Avenue, New York, New York 10016

Oxford is a registered trademark of Oxford University Press
All rights reserved. No part of this publication may be reproduced,
stored in a retrieval system, or transmitted, in any form or by any means,
electronic, mechanical, photocopying, recording or otherwise,
without the prior permission of Oxford University Press.

Library of Congress Cataloging-in-Publication Data
Ibn Gabirol, ca. 1022–ca. 1070.
[Keter malkhut.   English & Hebrew]
A crown for the king / Solomon ibn Gabirol : translated by David
R. Slavitt.
p.   cm.
Includes bibliographical references.
ISBN 0-19-511962-2
I. Slavitt, David R., 1935–   .
PJ5050.I3K413   1998
892.4'12—dc20   97-42452

1 3 5 7 9 8 6 4 2

Printed in the United States of America
on acid-free paper

For Samuel and Shoshana

PREFACE

S OLOMON IBN GABIROL (1021/2–ca. 1058) preceded his
better known Persian contemporary, 'Umar ibn Khayyam
(1048–1131), by only a few decades. The greatest of the Spanish
Jewish poets, Ibn Gabirol was also a neoplatonist philosopher
of prime importance. He wrote his poetry in Hebrew, which
was the sacramental language, and his prose works in Arabic.
Of the latter, three have survived: *The Book of Improvement
of Moral Qualities*, a guide to questions of ethics and education
with reference to the five senses and the four humors of an-
cient medicine; *The Choice of Pearls*, an anthology of ethical
maxims and proverbs; and his chief philosophical work, *The
Source of Life*, the original of which was lost. It was, however,
translated into Hebrew—*Meqor Hayim*—and then, in the

middle of the twelfth century, into Latin at the order of the Archbishop of Toledo by John of Seville, a converted Jew, and Dominicus Gundissalvus, the archdeacon of Segovia. That work—*Fons Vitae*, as it is called in Latin—became an influential text in the scholastic world. And just as "Ibn Sina" was turned by Latin writers into Avicena and Ibn Roshd transformed to Averroes, so Ibn Gabirol became known, variously, as Avencebrol, Avicembron, and Avicebron.

The medieval Christian scholastics who studied his philosophical ideas had no notion that he was a Jew celebrated as a writer of poetry used in the liturgy. (Passages of his work appear in the prayerbooks that are used today by Sephardic Jews.) It was only in 1846 that Solomon Munk, in *Literaturblatt des Orients*, announced that Avicebron was identical to Solomon ibn Gabirol.

Born in Malaga, Ibn Gabirol spent much of his life in Saragossa where his patron was Yequthiel ibn Hasan al-mutawakkil ibn Kabrun, a Jew who held a position at the Muslim court of Mundhir II. His poetry makes it clear that he suffered from a disfiguring dermatological ailment, perhaps furunculosis or tuberculosis of the skin. There were inevitable psychological consequences to this affliction and even Biblical resonances. Boils are the seventh plague. Even today, physicians sometimes refer to one form of furunculosis as "Job's disease." In one of his poems, Ibn Gabirol alludes to his sadness at his inability to participate in congregational worship, which is a vital aspect of Jewish prayer, and his disfiguring malady may well have been the cause of this very serious exclusion.

Solitary contemplation and private prayer, being less formulaic, is less likely to be disciplined. The extremes of emotion he reached in his solitude suggest the spiritual exercises of Rebbe Nachman of Bratslav who, eight centuries later, found in his "broken-heartedness" a doorway to the divine. Rebbe Nachman assumed that man's yearning for God was a reflection of God's for man. There is in Ibn Gabirol's poetry that same yearning and an extravagance, perhaps even a sublimated eroticism. The result is poetry with a unique combination of intimacy and power.

The theme of Ibn Gabirol's *Royal Crown* (Kether Malkhuth) is nothing less than the classic human predicament: man's frailty and proclivity to sin, and his place in a world in which providence is benign but must leave room for the operation of free will. We sin, but we are not excluded from the possibility of divine love because there always remains the opportunity of penitence and the unfathomable mystery of God's mercy. His cosmology uses elements of both the Jewish and Islamic traditions with certain Hellenistic influences. Bernard Lewis observes that he was very probably familiar with the work of Ibn Masarra (883–931) through whom

> ideas attributed to Empedocles and based on the teachings of Philo, Plotinus, Porphyrius, and Proclus became influential in medieval Spain. Ibn Masarra developed the doctrine of a "spiritual matter," common to all beings other than God, which he considers as the first hypostasis of the intelligible world. This, with an adaptation of the doctrine of emanations, is fundamental to the thought of Ibn Gabirol. It was to have considerable influence on subsequent Jewish religious thought,

both among the theologians, and, still more, among the Kabbalists.*

Moses ibn Ezra (c. 1055–after 1135), another eminent Jewish poet and critic, says of Ibn Gabirol:

> He was a craftsman who attained perfection in the use of language—one who had achieved mastery of what constitutes the aim of all poetry. . . . His way of handling metaphysical themes resembles that of the later Muslim poets and it earned him a reputation as a lord of language and prince of poetry. . . . Anyone who makes an intensive study of his poetry . . . learns to appreciate the power of its allusiveness to the Torah and the body of rabbinical tradition.

That phrase, "prince of poetry," was perhaps a way of Ibn Ezra's acknowledging or playfully exploiting the confusion that arose from *Shlomo malaqi* (Solomon of Malaga) with *Shlomo hamelekh* (king).

THERE IS ONE LITERARY STRATEGY in *A Crown for the King* that may require a word or two of explanation. Throughout the poem there are phrases and sentences from the *tanakh*, sometimes in contexts that are altogether different from their original settings in the Bible. There is, in the Western tradition, the cento, a kind of poem that does this feat of linguistic allograft for comic effect. Ausionius's pastiche of Virgilian lines and half lines, which he transforms into a ribald epithalamion, is perhaps the best known Latin cento, but there are others. And the aim is to show off the poet's learning while flattering and startling the reader, who recognizes the source, remembers the

*London: Valentine Mitchell, 1961. *The Kingly Crown*.

meaning of the quotation, and is amused or shocked by its reappearance in an altogether different context.

This technique is not usually intended as a serious spiritual exercise, but that, I am sure, is Ibn Gabirol's purpose. The multivalence of language can be a source of fun (as in the crudest pun) or an occasion for awe and majesty. The meanings of the words of the *tanakh* are inexhaustible. There is a saying that "Each man has his own Torah," which only begins to suggest the reverence Jews have had for the words of scripture and their belief in its richness. Ibn Gabirol's grand scheme is to provide a demonstration of how all the systems we might characterize as independent—the planets and other natural matter; Torah; God's will at work in the world—are really one system whose source is the One. His method is to give us a unique persona to guide our visions and through that persona to allegorize—to map all these systems one on top of the other.

The recognizable phrases that come floating across the consciousness of this persona are not just words but events in a life, the meaning of which is continually revealed retrospectively and enriched, as more and more connections make themselves clear.

I have not been able to reproduce every Biblical echo in Ibn Gabirol's poem, but I have indicated at least a few of them; enough, I hope, to show how the method works. It amounts to a peculiar and personal exegesis and is therefore altogether different, in intention, from the classical cento. The point is not to diminish and deflate the original phrases but to enlarge and elevate the speech of the poet who brings these phrases to bear on whatever comes to his attention. "These fragments have I shored against my ruin," is Eliot's phrase in "The Waste Land," and in his practice, which is not altogether dissimilar, the use of quotations and allusions has a fervor, even a desperation, that is close to the Gabirolian spirit.

A CROWN FOR THE KING

A Crown for the King

I pray that these my prayers may benefit man
and that he may learn the blessing of righteousness,
for I sing of the living God and his ways, a wonder.
I offer a taste, a glimpse, and my heart bears witness
here in my praise of the Lord, "a Crown for the King."

I

In the depths of my soul, I know: your works are great, and
　　your strength and glory and beauty and splendor.
Yours, O God, is the Kingdom and yours is the exaltation,
　　the riches, the honor due the magnificent ruler of higher
　　and lower creatures who all bear witness, perishing,
　　every one, while still you endure.
Yours is the limitless power that puzzles our minds: we try
　　to conceive it but cannot, such is its greatness.
Yours is the secret of secrets: your love of creation, the
　　yearning of all the forms for material being, your love,
　　that is, of your creatures, of us.

50

כֶּתֶר מַלְכוּת

בִּתְפִלָּתִי יִסְכָּן דָּבָר
כִּי בָהּ יְלַמַּד יֹשֶׁר חֲכוֹת:
סִפַּרְתִּי בָהּ פִּלְאֵי אֵל חָי
בִּקְצָרָה אַךְ לֹא בַאֲרִיכוּת:
שַׂמְתִּיהָ עַל רֹאשׁ מַהֲלָלַי   5
וּקְרָאתִיהָ כֶּתֶר מַלְכוּת:

א

נִפְלָאִים מַעֲשֶׂיךָ וְנַפְשִׁי יוֹדַעַת מְאֹד;

לְךָ יְיָ הַגְּדֻלָּה וְהַגְּבוּרָה וְהַתִּפְאֶרֶת וְהַנֵּצַח וְהַהוֹד:

לְךָ יְיָ הַמַּמְלָכָה וְהַמִּתְנַשֵּׂא לְכֹל לְרֹאשׁ וְהָעֹשֶׁר וְהַכָּבוֹד:

לְךָ בְּרוּאֵי מַעְלָה וּמַטָּה יָעִידוּ כִּי הֵמָּה יֹאבֵדוּ וְאַתָּה   10
תַעֲמֹד:

לְךָ הַגְּבוּרָה אֲשֶׁר בְּסוֹדָהּ נִלְאוּ רַעְיוֹנֵינוּ לַעֲמֹד. כִּי
עָצַמְתָּ מִמֶּנּוּ מְאֹד:

לְךָ חֶבְיוֹן הָעֹז הַסּוֹד וְהַיְסוֹד:

Yours* is the name that not even wise men know;
yours is the might that maintains the world at the brink of
    nothingness;
yours is the power to bring into sudden glare whatever is
    hidden,
as yours is the loving-kindness that rules your creatures, to
    whom you extend, for those of us who fear you, the
    treasure of goodness.
Yours is the mystery no man can ever fathom, that eternal
    life no death or decay can menace.
Yours is the throne, higher than any emperor's, in your
    hidden dwelling place in the loftiest heights.
Yours is the existence from the shadow of whose light came
    those emanations through which every being was made.
We came into existence and breathed and exclaimed, "In
    his shadow will we live."**
Yours are the two different worlds: this one we inhabit, and
    the other to which we go in the hope of reward
    righteous men must have.
You have set it aside and keep it for them somewhere
    hidden away and we long for it all the more.

II

You are one, the first number that is the beginning of
    arithmetic and geometry's starting point.
You are one, and at the mystery of your oneness, the
    cleverest mathematicians are struck dumb and cannot
    reckon with you.

*cf I Chron. xxix 11–12.
**Lam. iv, 20.

לְךָ הַשֵּׁם הַנֶּעְלָם מִמְּתֵי חָכְמָה. וְהַכֹּחַ הַסּוֹבֵל הָעוֹלָם 15
עַל בְּלִימָה. וְהַיְכוֹלֶת לְהוֹצִיא לָאוֹר כָּל תַּעֲלוּמָה:

לְךָ הַחֶסֶד אֲשֶׁר גָּבַר עַל בְּרוּאֶיךָ. וְהַטּוֹב הַצָּפוּן
לִירֵאֶיךָ:

לְךָ הַסּוֹדוֹת אֲשֶׁר לֹא יְכִילֵם שֵׂכֶל וְרַעְיוֹן. וְהַחַיִּים
אֲשֶׁר לֹא יִשְׁלַט עֲלֵיהֶם כִּלָּיוֹן. וְהַכִּסֵּא הַנַּעֲלָה עַל כָּל 20
עֶלְיוֹן. וְהַנָּוֶה הַנִּסְתָּר בְּרוּם חֶבְיוֹן:

לְךָ הַמְּצִיאוּת אֲשֶׁר מִצֵּל מְאוֹרוֹ נִהְיָה כָל הֹוֶה. אֲשֶׁר
אָמַרְנוּ בְּצִלּוֹ נִחְיֶה.

לְךָ שְׁנֵי הָעוֹלָמִים אֲשֶׁר נָתַתָּ בֵּינֵיהֶם גְּבוּל. הָרִאשׁוֹן
לְמַעֲשִׂים וְהַשֵּׁנִי לִגְמוּל: 25

לְךָ הַגְּמוּל אֲשֶׁר גָּנַזְתָּ לַצַּדִּיקִים וַתַּעֲלִימֵהוּ. וַתֵּרָא אֹתוֹ
כִּי טוֹב הוּא וַתִּצְפְּנֵהוּ:

ב

אַתָּה אֶחָד. רֹאשׁ כָּל מִנְיָן. וִיסוֹד כָּל בִּנְיָן:

אַתָּה אֶחָד. וּבְסוֹד אַחְדוּתְךָ חַכְמֵי לֵב יִתָּמֵהוּ. כִּי לֹא
יָדְעוּ מַה הוּא: 30

5

You are one in a oneness that, being all, cannot be enlarged
   or diminished from being to non-being. No fraction is
   missing and nothing is superfluous.
You are one but not that one an accountant tots up, or a
   broker, for you are not owned and you never fluctuate.
   You do not change in your attributes or form.
You are one, and yet no equation contains you. I cannot
   find the formula, chart, or table to calculate your
   proportions or dimensions. My mind fails, and therefore
   I say with the Psalmist, "I will guard my ways and try
   not to sin with my tongue."*
You are one, exalted, high above height, but not with the
   height of men from which we can fall, for how, and to
   what, and to where could the one fall?

III

You exist, but the keenest ear strains in the silence; the
   sharpest eye peers in the deep darkness; the mind tries to
   reason the how and why and fails.
You exist, but only for yourself, for your own essence:
   nothing comes near.
You exist: you are and always were, even before the
   beginning of time. You are everywhere, beyond all
   space.
You exist, but your mystery is perfect, for who can solve it?
   The preacher says, "It is far, far off, and very deep, and
   who can find it out?"**

**Ps. 39.
*Eccles. vii, 24.

6

אַתָּה אֶחָד. וְאַחְדוּתְךָ לֹא יִגָּרַע וְלֹא יוֹסִיף. לֹא יֶחְסַר
וְלֹא יַעֲדִיף:

אַתָּה אֶחָד. וְלֹא כְאֶחָד הַקָּנוּי וְהַמָּנוּי. כִּי לֹא יַשִּׂיגְךָ
רִבּוּי וְשִׁנּוּי. לֹא תֹאַר וְלֹא כִנּוּי:

35 אַתָּה אֶחָד. וְלָשׂוּם לְךָ חֹק וּגְבוּל נִלְאָה הֶגְיוֹנִי. עַל כֵּן
אָמַרְתִּי אֶשְׁמְרָה דְרָכַי מֵחֲטוֹא בִלְשׁוֹנִי:

אַתָּה אֶחָד. גָּבַהְתָּ וַתַּעֲלִיתָ מִשְּׁפוֹל וּמִנְּפוֹל. וְאִילוּ
הָאֶחָד שֶׁיִּפּוֹל:

ג

אַתָּה נִמְצָא. וְלֹא יַשִּׂיגְךָ שֵׁמַע אֹזֶן וְלֹא רְאוּת עַיִן. וְלֹא
40 יִשְׁלַט בְּךָ אֵיךְ וְלָמָּה וְאָיִן:

אַתָּה נִמְצָא. אֲבָל לְעַצְמָךְ וְאֵין לְאַחֵר עִמָּךְ:

אַתָּה נִמְצָא. וּבְטֶרֶם הֱיוֹת כָּל זְמָן הָיִיתָ. וּבְלִי מָקוֹם
חָנִיתָ:

אַתָּה נִמְצָא. וְסוֹדְךָ נֶעְלָם וּמִי יַשִּׂיגֶנּוּ. עָמוֹק עָמוֹק מִי
45 יִמְצָאֶנּוּ:

IV

You live, but not in time, for you are time itself.

You live but not by breathing in and breathing out, for you are breath itself.

You live, but not with a soul, for you are the source of souls.

You live but not with the life of man that is like vanity and ends in the ravening of worms and moths.

You live, and he who finds you out as you gather him into your eternal bliss "will eat and live forever."*

V

You are great, grand, huge, large, big. Compared with your greatness, all other greatness is cut down to size, mere pretension, a display not of merit and virtue but of shortcomings and tawdry failures.

You are great, so far beyond the concept of greatness that the beggared word profanes itself. Those starry heavens through which Ezekiel's chariot blazed are a sorry display.

You are great, surpassing grandeur and majesty; you are "exalted above all blessing and praise."**

VI

You are mighty: none of your creatures can match or imagine your great works and doughty deeds.

You are mighty with a perfect strength that never quavers or changes.

You are mighty but from your citadel of power can, in your moment of anger, forgive, for

*Gen. iii, 22.
**Neh. ix, 5.

8

ד

אַתָּה חַי. וְלֹא מִזְמָן קָבוּעַ. וְלֹא מֵעַת יָדוּעַ:

אַתָּה חַי. וְלֹא בְנֶפֶשׁ וּנְשָׁמָה כִּי אַתָּה נְשָׁמָה לִנְשָׁמָה:

אַתָּה חַי. וְלֹא כְּחַיֵּי אָדָם לַהֶבֶל דָּמָה. וְסוֹפוֹ עָשׁ
וְרִמָּה:

50　אַתָּה חַי. וְהַמַּגִּיעַ לְסוֹדְךָ יִמְצָא תַּעֲנוּג עוֹלָם. וְאָכַל
וָחַי לְעוֹלָם:

ה

אַתָּה גָדוֹל. וּמוּל גְּדֻלָּתְךָ כָּל גְּדֻלָּה נִכְנַעַת. וְכָל יִתְרוֹן
מִגְרָעַת:

אַתָּה גָדוֹל. מִכָּל מַחֲשָׁבָה. וְנָאֶה מִכָּל מֶרְכָּבָה:

55　אַתָּה גָדוֹל. עַל כָּל גְּדֻלָּה. וּמְרוֹמָם עַל כָּל תְּהִלָּה:

ו

אַתָּה גִבּוֹר. וְאֵין בְּכָל יְצִירוֹתֶיךָ וּבְרִיּוֹתֶיךָ אֲשֶׁר יַעֲשֶׂה
כְּמַעֲשֶׂיךָ וְכִגְבוּרוֹתֶיךָ:

אַתָּה גִבּוֹר. וּלְךָ הַגְּבוּרָה הַגְּמוּרָה. אֲשֶׁר אֵין לָהּ שִׁנּוּי
וּתְמוּרָה:

60　אַתָּה גִבּוֹר. וּמֵרוֹב גַּאֲוָתְךָ תִּמְחוֹל בְּעֵת זַעְפְּךָ. וְתַאֲרִיךְ
לְחַטָּאִים אַפְּךָ:

you are mighty in your mercy that softens your wrath
against sinners. That sweet pity of yours that rains down
upon all your creatures is "the mighty one of old."*

VII

You are light, but only the eyes of the pure of soul shall
behold you, for the clouds of sin shall obscure you from
sinners' eyes.

You are light that is everywhere, hidden in this world and
yet revealed in heaven, for "On the mount of the Lord
shall it be seen."**

You are light that is eternal: the intellect's eye that was
made to behold you and yearns for you catches only
glimmerings, but all of you we cannot see: it is at once
so glorious and blinding.

VIII

You are the God of gods, the Lord of lords, the ruler of all
beings of heaven and earth.

You are God, and all creatures testify to your greatness and
honor and everything you have made is bound to praise
your name and serve you.

You are God, and all creatures are your abject worshippers:
even those who worship other gods worship you, for
you are the one they long for.

*Gen. vi, 4.
**Gen. xxii, 14.

אַתָּה גִבּוֹר. וְרַחֲמֶיךָ עַל כָּל בְּרוּאֶיךָ כֻּלָּם. הֵמָּה
הַגְּבוּרִים אֲשֶׁר מֵעוֹלָם:

ז

אַתָּה אוֹר עֶלְיוֹן וְעֵינֵי כָל נֶפֶשׁ זַכָּה יִרְאוּךָ. וְעַנְנֵי עָוֹנִים
65 מֵעֵינֶיהָ יַעְלִימוּךָ:

אַתָּה אוֹר נֶעְלָם בָּעוֹלָם הַזֶּה וְנִגְלָה בָּעוֹלָם הַנִּרְאָה.
בְּהַר יְיָ יֵרָאָה:

אַתָּה אוֹר עוֹלָם. וְעֵין הַשֵּׂכֶל לְךָ תִּכְסוֹף וְתִשְׁתָּאֶה.
אֶפֶס קָצֵהוּ תִרְאֶה וְכֻלּוֹ לֹא תִרְאֶה:

ח

70 אַתָּה הוּא אֱלֹהֵי הָאֱלֹהִים וַאֲדוֹנֵי הָאֲדוֹנִים. שַׁלִּיט
בָּעֶלְיוֹנִים וּבַתַּחְתּוֹנִים:

אַתָּה אֱלֹהַּ. וְכָל הַבְּרוּאִים עֵדֶיךָ. וּבִכְבוֹד זֶה הַשֵּׁם
נִתְחַיַּב כָּל נִבְרָא לְעָבְדָךְ:

אַתָּה אֱלֹהַּ. וְכָל הַיְצוּרִים עֲבָדֶיךָ וְעוֹבְדֶיךָ. וְלֹא יֶחְסַר
76 כְּבוֹדֶךָ. בִּגְלַל עוֹבְדֵי בִלְעָדֶיךָ. כִּי כַוָּנַת כֻּלָּם לְהַגִּיעַ
עָדֶיךָ:

But they are like blind men who grope along the road.

One falls into the ditch of ruin and another stumbles into
    the abyss, and even as they fall, they insist they are going
    the right way.

Your servants, clear sighted, walk a straight path wavering
    neither to left nor right on a progress toward the castle
    of the king.

You are God, and your Godhead sustains your creatures
    with your oneness.

You are God, and there is no difference between your
    Godhead and your oneness, your always-have-been and
    your always-will-be,

for it is all the same mystery and though there are different
    names, they "all go to one place."*

IX

You are wise, and wisdom which is the source of life, arises
    from you, its source.

Men's wisdom is nothing: we are fools who cannot begin
    to imagine yours.

You are wise, the beginning of wisdom, for wisdom was
    born of you and nursed at your side.

You are wise but did not study under another, nor thought
    anything out or up, for it was always within.

*Eccles. iii, 20.

אֲבָל הֵם כְּעִוְרִים מְנַמַּת פְּנֵיהֶם דֶּרֶךְ הַמֶּלֶךְ . וְתָעוּ מִן
הַדָּרֶךְ :

זֶה טָבַע בִּבְאֵר שַׁחַת . וְזֶה נָפַל אֶל פָּחַת :

וְכֻלָּם חָשְׁבוּ כִּי לְחֶפְצָם נָּעוּ . וְהֵם לָרִיק יָגָעוּ : 80

אַךְ עֲבָדֶיךָ הֵם כִּפְקֻחִים . הַהוֹלְכִים דֶּרֶךְ נְכוֹחִים :

לֹא סָרוּ יָמִין וּשְׂמֹאל מִן הַדָּרֶךְ . עַד בּוֹאָם לַחֲצַר בֵּית
הַמֶּלֶךְ :

אַתָּה אֱלֹהַּ סוֹמֵךְ הַיְצוּרִים בֵּאלָהוּתָךְ . וְסוֹעֵד הַבְּרוּאִים
בְּאַחְדוּתָךְ : 85

אַתָּה אֱלֹהַּ . וְאֵין הַפְרֵשׁ בֵּין אֱלָהוּתָךְ וְאַחְדוּתָךְ .
וְקַדְמוּתָךְ וּמְצִיאוּתָךְ :

כִּי הַכֹּל סוֹד אֶחָד . וְאִם יִשְׁתַּנֶּה שֵׁם כָּל אֶחָד . הַכֹּל הוֹלֵךְ
אֶל מָקוֹם אֶחָד :

ט

אַתָּה חָכָם . וְהַחָכְמָה מְקוֹר חַיִּים מִמְּךָ נוֹבַעַת . וְחָכְמָתָךְ 90
נִבְעַר כָּל אָדָם מִדָּעַת :

אַתָּה חָכָם . וְקַדְמוֹן לְכָל קַדְמוֹן . וְהַחָכְמָה הָיְתָה אֶצְלָךְ
אָמוֹן :

אַתָּה חָכָם . וְלֹא לָמַדְתָּ מִבַּלְעָדֶיךָ . וְלֹא קָנִיתָ חָכְמָה
מִזּוּלָתָךְ : 95

You are wise, and from your wisdom came the creative
    will, the practiced knowledge of an artist's hand or a
    craftsman's that can sketch being on emptiness, can see
    objects into existence.
With no vessel you can draw light from the well of
    darkness, and with no tool you etch and polish, cleanse
    and refine.
The huge lump of nothing, you sundered to make the
    universe, and it unfolded, like cloud upon cloud in the
    heavens,
and that creative will, like a journeyman, fastened and
    measured and fit, and the pieces sprang together, like a
    nomad's tent going up, or the tent of the tabernacle,
and then a pavilion of tents stretching away to the horizon
    and beyond, "Linking the furthermost ends."*

X

Who can recount your unimaginable feats?
You made the globe of the earth and divided it, the dry
    land here and the water there.
And over the land and the water, you made a sphere of air,
    that atmosphere that turns as the world turns and rests on
    the world's turnings.
And over the air, you made the sphere of fire.

*Exod. xxxvi, 17.

אַתָּה חָכָם וּמַחְכְמָתְךָ אָצַלְתָּ חֵפֶץ מְזֻמָּן. כְּפֹעַל וְאָמָן:

לִמְשׁוֹךְ מֶשֶׁךְ הַיֵּשׁ מִן הָאַיִן. כְּהִמָּשֵׁךְ הָאוֹר הַיּוֹצֵא מִן
הָעָיִן:

וְשָׁאַב מִמְּקוֹר הָאוֹר מִבְּלִי דְלִי. וּפָעַל הַכֹּל בְּלִי כָלִי:

וְחָצַב וְחָקַק. וְטִהַר וְחָקַק: 100

וְקָרָא אֶל הָאַיִן וְנִבְקַע. וְאֶל הַיֵּשׁ וְנִתְקַע. וְאֶל הָעוֹלָם
וְנִרְקַע.

וְתִכֵּן שְׁחָקִים בַּזֶּרֶת. וְיָדוֹ אֹהֶל הַגַּלְגַּלִּים מְחַבָּרֶת.

וּבִלְלָאוֹת הַיְכוֹלֶת יְרִיעוֹת הַבְּרִיאוֹת קוֹשֶׁרֶת. וְכֹחָהּ
נוֹגַעַת עַד שְׂפַת הַבְּרִיאָה הַשְּׁפָלָה הַחִיצוֹנָה הַיְרִיעָה   105
הַקִּיצוֹנָה בַּמַּחְבָּרֶת:

מִי יְמַלֵּל גְּבוּרוֹתֶיךָ. בַּעֲשׂוֹתְךָ כַּדּוּר הָאָרֶץ נֶחֱלָק
לִשְׁנַיִם. חֶצְיוֹ יַבָּשָׁה וְחֶצְיוֹ מָיִם.

וְהִקַּפְתָּ עַל הַמַּיִם גַּלְגַּל הָרוּחַ. סוֹבֵב סוֹבֵב הוֹלֵךְ הָרוּחַ.
וְעַל סְבִיבוֹתָיו יָנוּחַ.   110

וְהִקַּפְתָּ עַל הָרוּחַ גַּלְגַּל הָאֵשׁ:

But these four elements are one, for their source is one.

And from the one source they come forth to refresh
themselves. "And from there it was separated, and
became four heads."*

XI

Who can declare your greatness?

You circumscribed the sphere of fire with the sphere of the
sky in which the moon revolves, aspiring and glowing in
the splendor of the sun.

In twenty-nine days, she completes her orbit to begin again
on her appointed path.

The process is simple and yet complex, full of puzzles and
paradoxes—as for instance that her mass is one thirty-
ninth that of the earth.

By the will of her creator, she waxes, wanes, and then
renews herself, a constancy of change, as good and evil
wax and wane, disappear and reappear here in the
world—"to make known to the sons of men his mighty
acts."**

XII

Who can recite your praises?

When you made the moon, you arranged it as a device to
calculate the festivals and holy days, a way to keep track
of the days and years.

*Gen. ii, 10.
**Ps. cxlv, 12.

וְהַיְסוֹדוֹת הָאֵלֶּה אַרְבַּעְתָּם לָהֶם יְסוֹד אֶחָד. וּמוֹצָאָם
אֶחָד.

וּמִמֶּנּוּ יוֹצְאִים וּמִתְחַדְּשִׁים. וּמִשָּׁם יִפָּרֵד וְהָיָה לְאַרְבָּעָה
רָאשִׁים: 115

יא

מִי יֶחֱזֶה גְדֻלָּתְךָ בַּהֲקִיפְךָ עַל גַּלְגַּל הָאֵשׁ גַּלְגַּל הָרָקִיעַ
וּבוֹ הַיָּרֵחַ. וּמִזִּיו הַשֶּׁמֶשׁ שׁוֹאֵף חוֹרֵחַ.

וּבְתִשְׁעָה וְעֶשְׂרִים יוֹם יָסֹב גַּלְגַּלּוֹ. וְיַעֲלֶה דַּרְךָּ גְּבוּלוֹ.

וְסוֹדֶיהָ מֵהֶם פְּשׁוּטִים וּמֵהֶם עֲמֻקִּים. וְגוּפוֹ פָחוּת מִגּוּף
הָאָרֶץ כְּחֵלֶק מִתִּשְׁעָה וּשְׁלֹשִׁים חֲלָקִים. 120

וְהוּא מְעוֹרֵר מִדֵּי חֹדֶשׁ בְּחָדְשׁוֹ חִדּוּשֵׁי עוֹלָם וְקוֹרוֹתָיו.
וְטוֹבוֹתָיו וְרָעוֹתָיו. בִּרְצוֹן הַבּוֹרֵא אֹתוֹ לְהוֹדִיעַ לִבְנֵי
הָאָדָם גְּבוּרוֹתָיו:

יב

מִי יַזְכִּיר תְּהִלָּתְךָ. בַּעֲשׂוֹתְךָ הַיָּרֵחַ רֹאשׁ לְחֶשְׁבּוֹן
מוֹעֲדִים וּזְמַנִּים. וּתְקוּפוֹת וְאוֹתוֹת לְיָמִים וְשָׁנִים: 125

At night, the moon reigns, until she comes to term and her
  light is obscured,
and she hides herself in a cloak of darkness, concealing
  herself from the sun, the source of her light,
and on the fourteenth day of her cycle, if the sun and the
  moon are disposed on the line of the Dragon so that the
  earth comes between, then the moon shows no light,
  and her lamp for a time is extinguished.
Thus, the men and the nations of earth may know that the
  heavenly bodies, although they are glorious, have a
  judge above them, who orders them to his rule.
And after her fall, the moon rises again, and after her
  eclipse, she resumes her shining.
And if, at the end of the month, she joins with the sun on
  the line of the Dragon,
Then the moon can obscure the sun and hide it as a cloud
  would, and its radiance disappears from our sight,
so that all men and nations of earth may know that the
  kingdom is not with the hosts and legions of the skies,

בַּלַּיְלָה מֶמְשַׁלְתּוֹ. עַד בּוֹא עִתּוֹ.

וְתֶחְשַׁךְ יִפְעָתוֹ. וְיִתְכַּסֶּה מַעֲטֵה קַדְרוּתוֹ. כִּי מְאוֹר
הַשֶּׁמֶשׁ אוֹרָתוֹ:

וּבְלֵיל אַרְבָּעָה עָשָׂר אִם יַעַמְדוּ עַל קַו הַתְּלִי שְׁנֵיהֶם.

130 וְיַפְרִיד בֵּינֵיהֶם.

אָז הַיָּרֵחַ לֹא יַהֵל אוֹרוֹ. וְיֶדְעַךְ נֵרוֹ:

לְמַעַן דַּעַת כָּל עַמֵּי הָאָרֶץ כִּי בְרוּאֵי מַעְלָה אִם הֵם
יְקָרִים. עֲלֵיהֶם שׁוֹפֵט לְהַשְׁפִּיל וּלְהָרִים:

אַךְ יִחְיֶה אַחֲרֵי נָפְלוֹ. וְיָאִיר אַחֲרֵי אָפְלוֹ.

135 וּבְהִדָּבְקוֹ בְּסוֹף הַחֹדֶשׁ עִם הַחַמָּה.

אִם יְהִי תְּלִי בֵּינֵיהֶם. וְעַל קַו אֶחָד יַעַמְדוּ שְׁנֵיהֶם.

אָז יַעֲמֹד הַיָּרֵחַ לִפְנֵי הַשֶּׁמֶשׁ כְּעָב שְׁחוֹרָה. וְיַסְתִּיר מֵעֵין
כָּל רֹאֶיהָ מְאוֹרָהּ.

לְמַעַן יֵדְעוּ כָל רֹאֵיהֶם. כִּי אֵין הַמַּלְכוּת לִצְבָא הַשָּׁמַיִם
140 וְחֵילֵיהֶם.

but there is a master over them, who lights their lights or
    darkens them,
"for he the high official is watched by a higher and there
    are yet higher ones over them."*
And those who take the sun for their god will be ashamed
    of what they have believed as their tenets are proven
    wrong,
for they will know that the hand of God made all this, and
    that the sun has no power of its own but he who
    darkened it is the powerful one,
sending to it a slave of one of his slaves, one who had
    benefited from its own light
to darken it for a time, to end the benightedness of idolatry
    and "remove him from being king."**

XIII

Who can appreciate adequately the accomplishment of your
    calculations?
You encompass the firmament of the moon with a further
    sphere without flaw or seam,
and in that sphere is the star we call Mercury, which is one
    twenty-two thousandth of the mass of the earth.
It whips around its orbit in ten months, causing on earth
    hatred's quarrels and strife, the harsh cries of invective
    and complaint,

*Eccles. v, 8.
**1 Kings xv, 13.

אֲבָל יֵשׁ אָדוֹן עֲלֵיהֶם. מַחֲשִׁיךְ מְאוֹרֵיהֶם.

כִּי נָבֹהַ מֵעַל גָּבֹהַּ שֹׁמֵר וּגְבֹהִים עֲלֵיהֶם. וְהַחוֹשְׁבִים
כִּי הַשֶּׁמֶשׁ אֱלֹהֵיהֶם.

בָּעֵת הַזֹּאת יֵבֹשׁוּ מִמַּחְשְׁבוֹתֵיהֶם. וְיִבָּחֲנוּ דִבְרֵיהֶם.

וְיָדְעוּ כִּי יַד יְיָ עָשְׂתָה זֹּאת וְאֵין לַשֶּׁמֶשׁ יְכֹלֶת. וְהַמַּחֲשִׁיךְ   145
אוֹרָהּ לוֹ לְבַדּוֹ הַמֶּמְשָׁלֶת.

וְהוּא הַשּׁוֹלֵחַ אֵלֶיהָ עֶבֶד מֵעֲבָדֶיהָ גְּמוּל חֲסָדֶיהָ.
לְהַסְתִּיר אוֹרָהּ. וְלִכְרוֹת מִפְלַצְתָּהּ וַיְסִירֶהָ מִגְּבִירֶהָ:

יג

מִי יְסַפֵּר צִדְקוֹתֶיךָ. בְּהַקִּיפְךָ עַל רְקִיעַ הַיָּרֵחַ גַּלְגַּל
שֵׁנִי בְּאֵין יוֹצֵאת וָפָרֶץ: 150

וּבוֹ כוֹכָב הַנִּקְרָא כוֹכָב וּמִדָּתוֹ כְּחַלָּק מִשְּׁנַיִם וְעֶשְׂרִים
אֶלֶף מִן הָאָרֶץ.

וּמַקִּיף הַגַּלְגַּל בַּעֲשָׂרָה יָמִים בְּמָרֶץ:

וְהוּא מְעוֹרֵר בָּעוֹלָם רִיבוֹת וּמְדָנִים. וְאֵיבוֹת וּרְגָנִים:

but it also gives powers for mastery over men and the
heaping up of wealth, the acquisition of treasure and
honor.

In doing this, it follows instructions, as a minister serves his
lord or as a slave obeys his master,

for it is a star of prudence and wisdom "to give subtlety to
the simple, and to the young man knowledge and
discretion."*

XIV

Who can understand your mysteries?

You encompassed the second sphere with a third in which
Venus reigns like a queen among her regiments, or a
bride among her bridesmaids.

It takes eleven months for her to complete her orbit, and
her mass is a thirty-seventh of that of the earth, the
scientists say.

By her creator's will, she renews the world,

brings peace, prosperity, dancing, and happiness, songs of
delight, shouts of joy,

and the cries of pleasure of the bride and groom in their
chamber.

Under her influence, sweet fruits and grains ripen, "the
precious fruits brought forth by the sun and the precious
things put forth by the moon."**

*Prov. i, 4.
**Deut. xxxiii, 14.

וְנוֹתֵן כֹּחַ לַעֲשׂוֹת חַיִל וְלִצְבּוֹר הוֹן. וְלִכְנוֹס עשֶׁר
וּמָמוֹן.

בְּמִצְוַת הַבּוֹרֵא אוֹתוֹ לְשָׁרְתוֹ כְּעֶבֶד לִפְנֵי אָדוֹן:

וְהוּא כּוֹכַב הַשֵּׂכֶל וְהַחָכְמָה.

נוֹתֵן לִפְתָאִים עָרְמָה. לְנַעַר דַּעַת וּמְזִמָּה:

יד

מִי יָבִין סוֹדוֹתֶיךָ. בְּהַקִּיפְךָ עַל גַּלְגַּל הַשֵּׁנִי גַּלְגַּל שְׁלִישִׁי
וּבוֹ נֹגַהּ כִּגְבֶרֶת בֵּין חֲיָלֶיהָ. וְכַכַּלָּה תַּעֲדֶה כֵלֶיהָ:

וּבְעַשְׁתֵּי עָשָׂר חֹדֶשׁ תָּסֹב גְּלִילֶיהָ. וְגוּפָהּ כְּחַלָּק מְשֻׁבְעָה
וּשְׁלֹשִׁים מִן הָאָרֶץ לְיוֹדְעֵי סֵדֶר הָ וּמַשְׂכִּילֶיהָ:

וְהִיא מְחֻדֶּשֶׁת בָּעוֹלָם כִּרְצוֹן בּוֹרְאָהּ.

הַשְׁקֵט וְשַׁלְוָה. וְדִיצָה וְחֶדְוָה:

וְשִׁירוֹת וּרְנָנִים. וּמִצְהָלוֹת חֲפוֹת חֲתָנִים.

וְהִיא מְקַשֶּׁרֶת פְּרִי תְנוּבוֹת וּשְׁאָר הַצְּמָחִים. מִמֶּגֶד
תְּבוּאוֹת שָׁמֶשׁ. וּמִמֶּגֶד גֶּרֶשׁ יְרָחִים:

XV

Who can fathom the enigma of your design?

You encompassed the sphere of Venus with a fourth sphere, that of the sun.

It completes its orbit in a year exactly.

Its mass, according to the calculations of astronomers and physicists, is a hundred seventy times that of the earth.

It radiates light through all of heaven and represents majesty and awe, which is to say the beginning of repentence.

It refreshes the miracles of the earth, sometimes fomenting war, sometimes bringing an end to war.

Its passage can uproot mighty kingdoms.

It has the power to raise up or dash down, according to its purpose but always according to the will of its creator who invested it with his wisdom.

Every day, he inclines his head before his lord as he takes his appointed place.

At dawn he stands for the morning prayer and for the evening prayer bows down to the west,

as is written in the Megillah of Esther: "In the evening she went, and in the morning she returned."*

*Esther ii, 14.

24

מִי יַשְׂכִּיל סוֹדְךָ בְּהַקִּיפְךָ עַל גַּלְגַּל נֹגַהּ גַּלְגַּל רְבִיעִי וּבוֹ
170 הַחַמָּה.

וְסוֹבֶבֶת כָּל הַגַּלְגַּל בְּשָׁנָה תְמִימָה.

וְגוּפָהּ גָּדוֹל מִגּוּף הָאָרֶץ מֵאָה וְשִׁבְעִים פַּעַם בְּמוֹפְתֵי
שֵׂכֶל וּמְזִמָּה.

וְהִיא חוֹלֶקֶת אוֹר לְכָל כּוֹכְבֵי שָׁמָיְמָה. וְנוֹתֶנֶת תְּשׁוּעָה
175 וְהוֹד מַלְכוּת וְאֵימָה.

וּמְחַדֶּשֶׁת נִפְלָאוֹת בָּעוֹלָם אִם לְשָׁלוֹם וְאִם לַמִּלְחָמָה.

וְעוֹקֶרֶת מַלְכִיּוֹת וְתַחְתָּם אֲחֵרוֹת מְקִימָה וּמְרִימָה.

וְלָהּ יְכֹלֶת לְהַשְׁפִּיל וּלְהָרִים בְּיָד רָמָה.

וְהַכֹּל בִּרְצוֹן הַבּוֹרֵא אוֹתָהּ בְּחָכְמָה:

180 וּבְכָל יוֹם נָיוֹם תִּשְׁתַּחֲוֶה לְמַלְכָּהּ וּבֵית נְצִיבוֹת נִצָּבָה.

וּבַשַּׁחַר תָּרִים רֹאשׁ וְתִקֹּד לָעֶרֶב בְּמַעֲרָבָהּ:

בָּעֶרֶב הִיא בָאָה וּבַבֹּקֶר הִיא שָׁבָה:

XVI

Who can grasp your magnificence?

You engineered the sun so that it tallies the days and the
    seasons

and the fruit trees come into blossom at the right time
        under the benevolent influence of the Pleiades and the
        belt of Orion.

For six months it goes north to warm the air, the waters
        and woods, and the bare rocks

as the farther north one goes the longer the days grow,

until, above the Arctic circle, there is a place where
        daylight goes on for months at a time,

but then, for six months, it journeys back to the south in its
        appointed course, and in that remote place in the Arctic,
        the night lasts for months and months.

This, at any rate, is what the geographers and cartographers
        tell us.

From them may be inferred a hint of the creator, a whisper
        of his mighty powers,

a hint of his strength and amazing accomplishments,

for from the greatness of the servant may the greatness of
        the master be calculated by men of judgment and
        understanding.

מִי יָכִיל גֻּדְלָתְךָ בַּעֲשׂוֹתְךָ אוֹתָהּ לִמְנוֹת בָּהּ יָמִים וְשָׁנִים.

וְעִתִּים מְזֻמָּנִים.

185 וּלְהַצְמִיחַ בָּהּ עֵץ עֹשֶׂה פְרִי וּמַעֲדַנֹּת כִּימָה וּמוֹשְׁכוֹת
כְּסִיל דְּשֵׁנִים וְרַעֲנַנִּים:

וְשִׁשָּׁה חֳדָשִׁים הוֹלָכַת לִפְאַת צָפוֹן לְחַמֵּם הָאַוּר וְהַמַּיִם
וְהָעֵצִים וְהָאֲבָנִים:

וּכְפִי קָרְבָתָהּ לַצָּפוֹן יִגְדְּלוּ הַיָּמִים וְיַאַרְכוּ הַזְּמַנִּים.

190 עַד יִמָּצֵא מָקוֹם אֲשֶׁר יִגְדַּל יוֹמוֹ עַד הֱיוֹתוֹ שִׁשָּׁה חֳדָשִׁים
בְּמוֹפְתִים נֶאֱמָנִים.

וְשִׁשָּׁה חֳדָשִׁים הוֹלָכַת לִפְאַת דָּרוֹם בְּמַעְגָּלִים נְתוּנִים.

עַד יִמָּצֵא מָקוֹם אֲשֶׁר יִנְדַּל לֵילוֹ עַד הֱיוֹתוֹ שִׁשָּׁה חֳדָשִׁים
לְפִי מִבְחַן הַבּוֹחֲנִים:

195 וּמִמֶּנָּה יָדְעוּ קְצָת דַּרְכֵי בוֹרְאָהּ וְשָׁמַץ מִגְּבוּרוֹתָיו.
וְעֻזּוֹ וְנִפְלְאוֹתָיו.

כִּי מִגְּדֻלַּת הָעֲבָדִים גְּדֻלַּת הָאָדוֹן נוֹדַעַת. לְכָל יוֹדְעֵי
דָעַת:

So, through the miracles of the sun's performance is
    revealed the even greater grandeur and glory of the
    Lord,
"for all the choice gifts of the master are in his hands."*

XVII

Who can read your riddles?
You have deputized the sun to provide light as the stars do,
    above and below, and to illuminate the moon which
    reflects his light like a bright mirror.
Even as she recedes from him, she takes his brilliance and it
    makes her face glow brighter and brighter
until she is opposite him and her entire visage shines back
    in his direction.
But then, as she draws nearer again, she turns her face away,
    as she approaches his side.
She turns shy as her cycle ends, and she joins him and hides
    with him in a secret place for a day and an hour and a
    minute,
and then, renewed, she reappears as before, "as a
    bridegroom coming out of his chamber."**

*Gen. xxiv, 10.
**Ps. xix, 5.

וְעַל הָעֶבֶד יַעֲלֶה תֹּקֶף הָאָדוֹן וּכְבוֹדוֹ. וְכָל טוּב אֲדֹנָיו
בְּיָדוֹ:

יז

מִי יַכִּיר אוֹתוֹתֶיךָ. בְּהַפְקִידְךָ אוֹתָהּ לְהַעֲנִיק אוֹר
לְכֹכְבֵי מַעֲלָה וּמַטָּה גַּם לַלְּבָנָה. וְאִם תַּחְתֶּיהָ תַּעֲמֹד
הַבַּהֶרֶת לְבָנָה.

וּכְפִי אֲשֶׁר יִרְחַק מִמֶּנָּה הַיָּרֵחַ. מִזִּיוָהּ לוֹקֵחַ.

כִּי בְרָחֳקוֹ יִקְרַב לַעֲמוֹד נָכְחָהּ. וִיקַבֵּל זָרְחָהּ.

עַד יִמָּלֵא אוֹרוֹ בְּעָמְדוֹ לְפָנֶיהָ. וְהֵאִיר אֶל עֵבֶר פָּנֶיהָ:

וְכָל אֲשֶׁר יִקְרַב אַחַר חֲצִי הַחֹדֶשׁ אֵלֶיהָ. הוּא נוֹטֶה
מֵעָלֶיהָ.

וְיִרְחַק מֵעֲמוֹד נֶגְדָּהּ. וְיֵלֵךְ לְצִדָּהּ.

וְעַל כֵּן תֶּחְסַר אַדַּרְתּוֹ.

עַד כְּלוֹת חׇדְשׁוֹ וּתְקוּפָתוֹ. וְיָבֹא בִּגְבוּל שְׂפָתוֹ:

וּבְהִדָּבְקוֹ עִמָּהּ. יִסָּתֵר בְּמִסְתָּרִים. כְּפִי יוֹם וַחֲצִי שָׁעָה
וּרְגָעִים סְפוּרִים:

וְאַחֲרֵי כֵן יִתְחַדֵּשׁ וְיָשׁוּב לְקַדְמוּתוֹ. וְהוּא כְּחָתָן יוֹצֵא
מֵחֻפָּתוֹ:

29

XVIII

Who can comprehend your wonderful accomplishments?

You have encompassed the sphere of the sun with a further
sphere, the fifth, where Mars holds court like a king in
his palace.

His orbit takes him eighteen months to complete, and his
measure is one and five-eighths the mass of the earth:
such is his magnitude.

He is a fierce warrior with a red shield, and he stirs up wars
that bring death and destruction by fire and sword,

and the sap of fruit trees crackling to dryness and years of
want.

Destruction is his business, thunder, lightning, hailstones,
and men transfixed

by swords and spears that other men have brought against
them,

"for their feet run to commit evil and they hasten to shed
innocent blood."*

XIX

Who can find words to describe your astonishing
achievements?

You have encompassed the sphere of Mars with a sixth
sphere, vast and terrible, in which the righteous planet
spins, for he is Jupiter, whom we call *Sedek*.

*Isa. lix, 7.

יח

מִי יָדַע פְּלִיאוֹתָיךְ בְּהַקִּיפְךָ עַל גַּלְגַּל חַמָּה גַּלְגַּל חֲמִישִׁי
וּבוֹ מַאְדִּים כְּמֶלֶךְ בְּהֵיכָלוֹ.

וּבִשְׁמוֹנָה עָשָׂר חֹדֶשׁ יֵטֹב גַּלְגַּלוֹ.

וּמִדָּתוֹ כְּגוּף הָאָרֶץ פַּעַם וָחֲצִי וּשְׁמִינִית פַּעַם וְזֶה תַכְלִית
220   גָדְלוֹ:

וְהוּא כְּגִבּוֹר עָרִיץ מָנֶן גְּבוּרֵיהוּ מְאָדָּם.

וּמְעוֹרֵר מִלְחָמוֹת וְהֶרֶג וְאַבְדָּן.

וּמִכְּבִי חֶרֶב וְלִחְמֵי רֶשֶׁף נֶהְפַּךְ לְחֹרֶב לְשַׁדָּם.

וְשָׁנוֹת בַּצֹּרֶת וּשְׂרֵפַת אֵשׁ וּרְעָמִים וְאַבְנֵי אֶלְגָּבִישׁ
225   וּמְדָקָרִים וּשְׁלוּפֵי חֶרֶב כְּנֶגְדָם.

כִּי רַגְלֵיהֶם לָרַע יָרוּצוּ וִימַהֲרוּ לִשְׁפָּךְ דָּם:

יט

מִי יַבִּיעַ נוֹרְאוֹתָיךְ בְּהַקִּיפְךָ עַל גַּלְגַּל מַאְדִּים גַּלְגַּל שִׁשִּׁי
הוֹלֵךְ בִּמְסִבָּה.

עֲצוּמָה וְרַבָּה.

230   צֶדֶק יָלִין בָּהּ.

His body is seventy-five times greater than that of the earth,
and he completes his orbit in twelve years.
He is a planet of *sedakah*, of righteousness, generosity and of
love, and he arouses an awe of heaven,
inspiring us to rectitude and repentance and encouraging
every good moral quality.
He also has a beneficent influence on crops of the fields and
fruits of the vines and the trees.
He pacifies men's hearts, soothing enmity and strife so that
wars can come to an end.
His appointed task is to repair what needs repairing, and fix
what needs fixing,
"for he judges the world in righteousness."*

XX

Who can follow your intricacies?
You encompassed the sphere of Jupiter with a seventh
sphere in which Saturn revolves
whose body is ninety-nine times greater than that of the
earth, and who completes his revolution in thirty years.
He stirs up wars and rapine and pillage and captivity and
brings famine, for such is his assignment,
and he overthrows kingdoms and devastates countries
according to the will of his master,
"who has appointed him to his service, even such strange
service."**

*Ps. xcviii, 9.
**Isa. xxviii, 21.

32

וְנוּפוֹ נָדוֹל מִגּוּף הָאָרֶץ חֲמִשָּׁה וְשִׁבְעִים פַּעַם בְּמִדַּת
רָחְבָּהּ.

וְסוֹבֵב הַגַּלְגַּל בִּשְׁתֵּים עֶשְׂרֵה שָׁנָה וְהוּא כּוֹכַב הָרָצוֹן
וְהָאַהֲבָה.

וּמְעוֹרֵר יִרְאַת הַשֵּׁם וְיֹשֶׁר וּתְשׁוּבָה.

וְכָל מִדָּה טוֹבָה.

וּמַרְבָּה כָּל תְּנוּבָה וּתְבוּאָה.

וּמַשְׁבִּית מִלְחָמוֹת וְאֵיבָה וּמְרִיבָה:

וְדָתוֹ לַחֲזַק בְּיָשְׁרוֹ כָּל בָּדָק. וְהוּא יִשְׁפֹּט תֵּבֵל בְּצֶדֶק:

כ

מִי יְשׂוֹחֵחַ גְּדֻלָּתְךָ בְּהַקִּיפְךָ עַל נַּלְנַּל צֶדֶק נַּלְנַּל שְׁבִיעִי
וּבוֹ שַׁבְתַּי בִּתְקוּפָתוֹ.

וְנוּפוֹ נָדוֹל מִגּוּף הָאָרֶץ אַחַת וְתִשְׁעִים פַּעַם בְּמִדָּתוֹ.

וְסוֹבֵב הַגַּלְגַּל בִּשְׁלֹשִׁים שָׁנָה בִּמְרוּצָתוֹ.

וּמְעוֹרֵר מִלְחָמוֹת וּבִזָּה וּשְׁבִי וְרָעָב כִּי כֵן דָּתוֹ.

וּמַחֲרִיב אֲרָצוֹת וְעוֹקֵר מַלְכֻיּוֹת בִּרְצוֹן הַמַּפְקִיד אוֹתוֹ
לַעֲבוֹד עֲבוֹדָתוֹ נָכְרִיָּה עֲבוֹדָתוֹ:

33

XXI

Who can even aspire to your loftiness?

You have encompassed the sphere of Saturn with an eighth
sphere where the twelve signs of the zodiac shine on the
belt of its priestly vestment and all the stars of high
heaven are fixed in their places,

each of those stars being a part of that sphere which is so
high that its orbit is thirty-six thousand years.

The bodies of those great stars are a hundred and seven
times the mass of the earth,

and from the power they exert come the forces that direct
our lives here below,

each according to its destiny and the will of its creator, who
disposed every one in its proper place, set its intended
course, and gave it a name, "each according to his
service and his burden."*

XXII

Who can follow your pathways?

For the seven planets you made palaces among the twelve
constellations, giving both to the Ram and the Bull the
gift of your strength, and to the Twins giving the faces
of men that face each other in brotherhood.

*Num. iv, 49.

34

כא

מִי יַגִּיעַ לִרוֹמְמוּתָךְ בְּהַקִּיפְךָ עַל גַּלְגַּל שַׁבְתַי גַּלְגַּל שְׁמִינִי
בְּמִסְבָּתוֹ.

וְהוּא סוֹבֵל שְׁתַּיִם עֶשְׂרֵה מַזָּלוֹת עַל קַו חֻשַּׁב אֲפֻדָּתוֹ.

וְכָל כֹּכְבֵי שַׁחַק הָעֶלְיוֹנִים יְצוּקִים בִּיצוּקָתוֹ.   250

וְכָל כּוֹכָב מֵהֶם יַקִּיף הַגַּלְגַּל בְּשִׁשָּׁה וּשְׁלשִׁים אֶלֶף שָׁנִים
מֵרֹב גָּבְהוּתוֹ.

וְגוּף כָּל כֹּכָב מֵהֶם מֵאָה וְשֶׁבַע פְּעָמִים כְּגוּף הָאָרֶץ
וְזֹאת תַּכְלִית גָּדְלָתוֹ:

וּמִכֹּחַ הַמַּזָּלוֹת הָהֵם. נֶאֱצַל כֹּחַ כָּל בְּרוּאֵי מַטָּה   255
לְמִינֵיהֶם. בִּרְצוֹן בּוֹרְאָם וּמַפְקִידָם עֲלֵיהֶם:

וְכָל אֶחָד מֵהֶם עַל מַתְכֻּנְתּוֹ בְּרָאוֹ. וּבְשֵׁם קְרָאוֹ. אִישׁ
אִישׁ עַל עֲבוֹדָתוֹ וְעַל מַשָּׂאוֹ:

כב

מִי יַדַע הֲלִיכוֹתֶיךָ בַּעֲשׂוֹתְךָ לְשִׁבְעָה כֹכְבֵי לָכַת
הֵיכָלוֹת. בִּשְׁתַּיִם עֶשְׂרֵה מַזָּלוֹת.   260

וְעַל טָלֶה וָשׁוֹר אָצַלְתָּ כֹחַ בְּהִתְיַחֲדָם. וְהַשְּׁלִישִׁי
תְּאוֹמִים כִּשְׁנֵי אַחִים בְּהִתְאַחֲדָם. וּדְמוּת פְּנֵיהֶם פְּנֵי אָדָם.

The fourth is Cancer the Crab, and him and the Lion you
   have endowed with splendor,
and splendor also have you given to his sister the Virgin.
You have disposed Libra and Scorpio at his sides
and Sagittarius who is mighty with the bow,
and your powers have created Capricorn and Aquarius and
   assigned them their places,
and then, at the last place, is the fish for, as it is written,
   "now the Lord had prepared a great fish."*
These are the constellations, noble and exalted, "twelve
   princes according to their tribes."**

XXIII

Who can grope his way into the depths of your secrets?
Beyond the sphere of the constellations, you have
   established a ninth sphere encompassing all the others
   and all the creatures enclosed within your creation.
This sphere governs all the stars in the skies in their orbits
   from east to west imparting motion to them.
Every day, it bows to the west to the King enthroned as its
   Lord.

*Jon. i, 17.
**Gen. xxv, 16.

וְלָרְבִיעִי וְהוּא סַרְטָן נֵם לְאַרְיֵה נָתַתָּ מַהוֹדְךָ עָלָיו.
וְלָאֲחוֹתוֹ הַבְּתוּלָה הַקְּרוֹבָה אֵלָיו.

וְכֵן לַמֹּאזְנַיִם וְלָעַקְרָב אֲשֶׁר בְּצִדּוֹ הוּשָׁת. וְהַתְּשִׁיעִי   265
הַגִּבְרָא בְּצוּרַת גִּבּוֹר כֹּחוֹ לֹא נָשָׁת. וַיְהִי רוֹבֶה קַשָּׁת.

וְכֵן נִבְרָא גְּדִי וּדְלִי בְּכֹחַךְ הַגָּדוֹל. וּלְבַדּוֹ הַמַּזָּל הָאַחֲרוֹן
וַיְמַן יְיָ דָּג גָּדוֹל:

וְאֵלֶּה הַמַּזָּלוֹת הַגְּבוֹהִים וְנִשָּׂאִים בְּמַעֲלוֹתָם. שְׁנַיִם עָשָׂר
נְשִׂיאִים לְאֻמּוֹתָם: 270

כג

מִי יַחְקוֹר תַּעֲלוּמוֹתֶיךָ בְּהַאֲצִילְךָ עַל גַּלְגַּל הַמַּזָּלוֹת
גַּלְגַּל תְּשִׁיעִי בְּמַעֲרָכוֹ.

הַמַּקִּיף עַל כָּל הַגַּלְגַּלִּים וּבְרוּאֵיהֶם וְהֵם סְגוּרִים
בְּתוֹכוֹ.

הַמַּנְהִיג כָּל כּוֹכְבֵי שָׁמַיִם וְגַלְגַּלֵּיהֶם מִמִּזְרָח לְמַעֲרָב   275
לְתֹקֶף מַהֲלָכוֹ.

הַמִּשְׁתַּחֲוָה פַּעַם בְּכָל יוֹם לִפְאַת מַעֲרָב לְמַלְכּוֹ
וּמַמְלִיכוֹ.

So vast is it that all the creatures of the universe are like a
    mustard seed floating in a mighty ocean,
but great as it is, it is as nothing before the greatness of its
    creator and its master, "counted by him as less than
    nothing and emptiness."*

XXIV

Who can understand your mysteries?
You raised up over the ninth sphere the sphere of
    Intelligence,
holy as the temple itself for, as it is written,
"and the tenth shall be holy unto the Lord."**
This is the sphere higher than height itself,
a thought that defies thinking, an idea too large for any
    mind to grasp,
for this is the mystery, the bridal canopy of your glory.
You made it from the silver of truth and fashioned its
    covering with the gold of wisdom.
You set its orbit on pillars of righteousness, and by your
    power called it all into existence.
It comes from you and it yearns toward you: "for you shall
    be its desire."***

XXV

Who can fathom your profundities?
From the splendor of the sphere of Intelligence, you made
    the radiance of souls,

*Isa. xl, 17.
**Lev. xxvii, 32.
***Gen. iv, 7.

וְכָל בְּרוּאֵי עוֹלָם בְּתוֹכוֹ.

כְּגַרְגִּיר חַרְדָּל בַּיָּם הַגָּדוֹל לְתֹקֶף גָּדְלוֹ וְעָרְכּוֹ. 280

וְהוּא וּגְדֻלָּתוֹ נֶחְשָׁב כְּאַיִן וּכְאֶפֶס לְגֻדְלַת בּוֹרְאוֹ וּמַלְכּוֹ:

וְכָל מַעֲלוֹתָיו וְנֶדְלוֹ. מֵאֶפֶס וָתֹהוּ נֶחְשְׁבוּ לוֹ:

כד

מִי יָבִין סוֹדוֹת בְּרִיאוֹתֶךָ בַּהֲרִימְךָ עַל גַּלְגַּל הַתְּשִׁיעִי
גַּלְגַּל הַשֵּׂכֶל הוּא הַהֵיכָל לְפָנָי. הָעֲשִׂירִי יִהְיֶה קֹדֶשׁ לַיְיָ:

וְהוּא הַגַּלְגַּל הַנַּעֲלָה עַל כָּל עֶלְיוֹן. אֲשֶׁר לֹא יְשִׂיגֵנְהוּ 285
רַעְיוֹן.

וְשָׁם הַחֲבִיוֹן. אֲשֶׁר הוּא לִכְבוֹדְךָ לְאַפִּרְיוֹן.

מִכֶּסֶף הָאֱמֶת יָצַקְתָּ אוֹתוֹ. וּמִזְּהַב הַשֵּׂכֶל עָשִׂיתָ רְפִידָתוֹ.

וְעַל עַמּוּדֵי צֶדֶק שַׂמְתָּ מְסִבָּתוֹ. וּמִכֹּחֲךָ מְצִיאוּתוֹ.

וּמִמְּךָ וְעָדֶיךָ מְנֻמָּתוֹ. וְאֵלֶיךָ תְּשׁוּקָתוֹ: 290

כה

מִי יַעֲמִיק לְמַחְשְׁבוֹתֶיךָ בַּעֲשׂוֹתְךָ מִזִּיו גַּלְגַּל הַשֵּׂכֶל זֹהַר
הַנְּשָׁמוֹת. וְהַנְּפָשׁוֹת הָרָמוֹת.

39

the messengers of your will, the ministers of your presence.
They are majestic in their strength and powerful in the
    kingdom of heaven.
"In their hand is the flaming sword that turns every way."*
They do whatever is necessary, wherever the spirit
    prompts.
These are the forms, the transcendent essences, shimmering
    like pearls.
These are the servants of the outer court, or angels of the
    inner chamber who gaze at you directly and attend upon
    you.
They arise from holiness and they are drawn from the
    source of light.
There are regiments of them, companies and battalions with
    their banners that the artists have designed.
Some give orders and others obey, and they run this way
    and that in unwearying activity seeing all but never seen.
Some are made of fire, and some are air, and some are fire
    and water compounded together.
The seraphs come in their burning rows, the leaping sparks,
    the flashes of lightning, the comets and meteors,
and every trooper of them bows down in obeisance "to
    him who rides the highest heavens."**
In the highest sphere of the universe they stand in their
    myriads and thousands of myriads, arranged in their
    squads and platoons.

*Gen. iii, 24.
**Ps. lxviii, 5.

הֵם מַלְאֲכֵי רְצוֹנֶךָ. מְשָׁרְתֵי פָנֶיךָ:

הֵם אַדִּירֵי כֹחַ וְגִבּוֹרֵי מַמְלָכָת. בְּיָדָם לַהַט הַחֶרֶב
הַמִּתְהַפָּכֶת. 295

וְעֹשֵׂי כָל מְלָאכֶת. אֶל אֲשֶׁר יִהְיֶה שָׁמָּה הָרוּחַ לָלָכֶת:

כֻּלָּם גְּזָרוֹת פְּנִינִיּוֹת וְחַיּוֹת עֶלְיוֹת. חִיצוֹנִיּוֹת וּפְנִימִיּוֹת.
הֲלִיכוֹתֶיךָ צוֹפִיּוֹת:

מִמְּקוֹם קָדוֹשׁ יְהַלֵּכוּ. וּמִמְּקוֹר הָאוֹר יְמַשְׁכוּ:

נֶחֱלָקִים לְכִתּוֹת. וְעַל דִּגְלָם אוֹתוֹת. 300

בְּעֵט סוֹפֵר מָהִיר חֲרוּתוֹת. מֵהֶם נְסִיכוֹת וּמֵהֶם
מְשָׁרְתוֹת:

מֵהֶם צְבָאוֹת. רָצוֹת וּבָאוֹת.

לֹא עֲיֵפוֹת וְלֹא נִלְאוֹת. רוֹאוֹת וְלֹא נִרְאוֹת:

מֵהֶם חֲצוּבֵי לֶהָבוֹת. וּמֵהֶם רוּחוֹת נוֹשְׁבוֹת. מֵהֶם מֵאֵשׁ 305
וּמִמַּיִם מָרְכָּבוֹת:

מֵהֶם שְׂרָפִים. וּמֵהֶם רְשָׁפִים.

מֵהֶם בְּרָקִים. וּמֵהֶם זִיקִים:

וְכָל כַּת מֵהֶם מִשְׁתַּחֲוָה לְרוֹכֵב עֲרָבוֹת. וּבְרוּם עוֹלָם
נִצָּבִים לַאֲלָפִים וְלִרְבָבוֹת: 310

Their watches change every day and night, and they mark
their vigils with the rituals of psalms and hymns to him
who is girded with strength.
All of them bow down in fear and trembling, kneeling
before you and lying prostrate, and confess to you
that "you are our God and you did make us, and we are
yours."* We are all the work of your hands,
for you are our God and we are your servants, you are our
creator, and we are the bearers of witness.

XXVI

Who can approach your dwelling place?
You raised up above the sphere of Intelligence your throne
of glory,
the mystic home of majesty, the secret and the
foundation—the forms, matter, and divine will.
Intelligence reaches out for it, stretching, yearning, but falls
far short.
Above it, you are raised up, exalted on your mighty throne,
"and no one shall come up with you."**

XXVII

Whose achievements can compare with yours?
At the foot of your throne of splendor you have made a
place for your saints' souls.

*Ps. c, 3.
**Exod. xxxiv, 3.

נֶחֱלָקִים לְמִשְׁמָרוֹת. בַּיּוֹם וּבַלַּיְלָה לְרֹאשׁ אַשְׁמוּרוֹת.

לַעֲרוֹךְ תְּהִלּוֹת וְשִׁירוֹת. לַנָּאְזָר בִּגְבוּרוֹת:

כֻּלָּם בַּחֲרָדָה וּרְעָדָה כּוֹרְעִים וּמִשְׁתַּחֲוִים לָךְ. וְאוֹמְרִים
מוֹדִים אֲנַחְנוּ לָךְ:

315 שָׁאַתָּה אֱלֹהֵינוּ. אַתָּה עֲשִׂיתָנוּ.

וְלֹא אֲנַחְנוּ. וּמַעֲשֵׂה יָדְךָ כֻּלָּנוּ:

וְכִי אַתָּה אֲדוֹנֵנוּ וַאֲנַחְנוּ עֲבָדֶיךָ. וְאַתָּה בוֹרְאֵנוּ וַאֲנַחְנוּ
עֵדֶיךָ:

כו

מִי יָבֹא עַד תְּכוּנָתֶךָ. בְּהַגְבִּיהֶךָ לְמַעְלָה מִגַּלְגַּל הַשֵּׂכֶל
320 כִּסֵּא הַכָּבוֹד. אֲשֶׁר שָׁם נְוֵה הֶחָבִיּוֹן וְהַהוֹד.

וְשָׁם הַסּוֹד וְהַיְסֹד. וְעָדָיו יַגִּיעַ הַשֵּׂכֶל וְיַעֲמֹד:

וּמִלְמַעְלָה נָאִיתָ וְעָלִיתָ עַל כֵּס תַּעֲצוּמֶךָ. וְאִישׁ לֹא
יַעֲלֶה עִמָּךְ:

כז

מִי יַעֲשֶׂה כְמַעֲשֶׂיךָ. בַּעֲשׂוֹתְךָ תַּחַת כִּסֵּא כְבוֹדֶךָ.
325 מַעֲמָד לְנַפְשׁוֹת חֲסִידֶיךָ:

43

There in the home for the pure of heart they are bound up
in the bundle of life.
Those who here are weary unto death await to find new
strength there,
and those who are faint may find rest and renewal there, for
they are the children of repose.
For them is delight beyond all bounds, happiness without
end, for this is the world to come
and there are places to stand and mirrors into which to look
to see the face of the Lord, and to be seen
in the palace of the King where they dwell forever,
at the King's banquet table nibbling the fruits of
intelligence, which are the royal sweetmeats.
This is their rest, their reward, and their inheritance
the goodness and beauty of which are limitless,
for here is "the land that flows with milk and honey and
this is its fruit."*

XXVIII

Who can count your wonders?
In the heights, you have made vaults full of riches,
and the whispers about them and the rumors are many and
strange.
In some of these treasuries, there is life everlasting for the
pure and the righteous,
and in some of the warehouses, there is salvation for those
who have sinned but repented.

*Num. xiii, 27.

Read sections at
1999 Kol Nidre,
at Harwin's house

tive on the union of body and soul allows

Knowing that it is a strictly natural,

attaching psychological anxieties to death.

anticipations. Understanding Lucretius'

one holds respect for nature, knowing that it

orce. Thus, the selfish fear of the

ear that all experiences will end, the fear of

ices for survivors all shall be overcome

caying is consoled when one understands

Everything is composed of atoms, and so the

aking one's body when one dies. One must

organic matter, and that one is part of that

y's inevitable dissolution, Segal says in

t understand that the human flesh is frail

man's soft skin and brittle bones are

The notion that disease and decay shall take

ncontrollable, chaotic forces that humans

book six of Lucretius' work illustrates the

f chaos engulfs the entire universe, as the

ites:

not just a displacement or projection of

on the natural world; it is also a

on the vast screen of the universe of the

וְשָׁם נְוֵה הַנְּשָׁמוֹת הַטְּהוֹרוֹת. אֲשֶׁר בִּצְרוֹר הַחַיִּים
צְרוּרוֹת:

וַאֲשֶׁר יִיגְעוּ וְיִיעָפוּ. שָׁם כֹּחַ יַחֲלִיפוּ.

וְשָׁם יָנוּחוּ יְגִיעֵי כֹחַ. וְאֵלֶּה בְּנֵי נֹחַ:

וּבוֹ נֹעַם בְּלִי תַכְלִית וְקִצְבָה. וְהוּא הָעוֹלָם הַבָּא: 330

וְשָׁם מַעֲמָדוֹת וּמַרְאוֹת. לַנְּפָשׁוֹת הָעוֹמְדוֹת בְּמַרְאוֹת
הַצּוֹבְאוֹת.

אֶת פְּנֵי הָאָדוֹן לִרְאוֹת וּלְהֵרָאוֹת:

שׁוֹכְנוֹת בְּהֵיכְלֵי מֶלֶךְ. וְעוֹמְדוֹת עַל שֻׁלְחַן הַמֶּלֶךְ.

וּמִתְעַדְּנוֹת בְּמֶתֶק פְּרִי הַשֵּׂכֶל וְהוּא יִתֵּן מַעֲדַנֵּי מָלֶךְ: 335

זֹאת הַמְּנוּחָה וְהַנַּחֲלָה אֲשֶׁר אֵין תַּכְלִית לְטוּבָהּ וְיָפְיָהּ
וְגַם זָבַת חָלָב וּדְבַשׁ הִוא וְזֶה־פִּרְיָהּ:

כח

מִי יַעֲלֶה צְפוּנוֹתֶיךָ בַּעֲשׂוֹתֶךָ בַּמָּרוֹם חֲדָרִים וְאוֹצָרוֹת.
בָּהֶם נוֹרָאוֹת סְפוּרוֹת. וּדְבַר גְּבוּרוֹת:

מֵהֶם אוֹצְרוֹת חַיִּים. לְזַכִּים וּנְקִיִּים: 340

וּמֵהֶם אוֹצְרוֹת יֶשַׁע. לְשָׁבֵי פָשַׁע:

In some, there are blazing fires and rivers of sulphur for
    those who have broken the covenant,
and in some there are pits that seethe and bubble endlessly:
"He that is abhorred of the Lord shall fall into it."*
There are caves full of winds and downpours, of hailstorms
    and sleet,
a wealth of snow, hoards of searing heat, troves of floods,
collections of clouds and thick smoke, and repositories of
    deep murk and darkness.
All these you have prepared and put by for their due
    seasons, and you keep them at hand
"You have ordained them as a judgment, and established
    them, O Rock, for chastisement."**

XXIX

Who can imagine your power?
From your abundant glory you created pure radiance, hewn
    from rock mined in the heart of the pit
and you imbued it with the life of wisdom and called it
    Soul.
You tempered it in the forge of intelligence so that its spirit
    glows and shimmers,

*Prov. xxii, 14.
**Hab. i, 12.

46

וּמֵהֶם אוֹצְרוֹת אֵשׁ וְנַחֲלֵי נָפְרִית. לְעוֹבְרֵי בְרִית:

וְאוֹצְרוֹת שׁוּחוֹת עֲמוּקוֹת לֹא תִכְבֶּה אִשָּׁם. וְעוֹם יְיָ יִפֹּל
שָׁם:

וְאוֹצְרוֹת סוּפוֹת וּסְעָרוֹת. וְקִפָּאוֹן וִיקָרוֹת: 345

וְאוֹצְרוֹת בָּרָד וָקֶרַח וָשֶׁלֶג וְצִיָּה גַם חֹם וְנוֹזְלֵי פָלָג:

וְקִיטוֹר וּכְפוֹר וְעָנָן וַעֲרָפֶל. וַעֲלָטָה וָאֹפֶל:

הַכֹּל הֲכִינוֹת בְּעִתּוֹ. אִם לְחֶסֶד אִם לְמִשְׁפָּט שַׂמְתּוֹ.

וְצוּר לְהוֹכִיחַ יְסַדְתּוֹ:

כט

מִי יָכִיל עָצְמָתָךְ בְּבָרְאֲךָ מִזִּיו כְּבוֹדְךָ יִפְעָה טְהוֹרָה.   350

מְצוּר הַצוּר נִגְזָרָה. וּמִמַּקֶּבֶת בּוֹר נְקָרָה:

וְאָצַלְתָּ עָלֶיהָ רוּחַ חָכְמָה. וְקָרָאתָ שְׁמָהּ נְשָׁמָה:

עֲשִׂיתָהּ מִלַּהֲבוֹת אֵשׁ הַשֵּׂכֶל הַצּוּרָה. וּנְשַׁפְתָּהּ כְּאֵשׁ
בּוֹעֲרָה.

and you invested it in the body that serves it and protects it,
for it is the fire that burns within but does not consume it.
From the spark of the spirit it came, from Nothingness to
  Being.
"because the Lord descended upon it in fire."*

XXX

Who can aspire to your wisdom?
You gave the soul the gift of knowledge and its power
  inheres in her.
Knowledge is the source of her glory, and therefore she
  cannot wither or decay but endures, as knowledge
  endures.
This is her nature and her mystery.
The soul with its wisdom cannot die, but for sin will she be
  punished with worse than death,
while the pure shall have grace and smile on the last day.
Defilement shall wander through storms of anger and hatred
and shall sit alone during all the days of her uncleanness,
an outlaw, an outcast, a captive, and a vagabond,
and "she shall touch no hallowed thing nor come into the
  sanctuary until the days of her purification are
  fulfilled."**

*Exod. xix, 18.
**Lev. xii, 4.

48

וְשָׁלַחְתָּה בַּגּוּף לְעָבְדֵהוּ וּלְשָׁמְרֵהוּ. וְהִיא כְּאֵשׁ בְּתוֹכוֹ 355
וְלֹא תִשְׂרְפֵהוּ.

כִּי מֵאֵשׁ הַנְּשָׁמָה נִבְרָא וְיָצָא מֵאַיִן לַיֵשׁ. מִפְּנֵי אֲשֶׁר יָרַד
עָלָיו יְיָ בָּאֵשׁ:

ל

מִי יַגִּיעַ לְחָכְמָתָךְ בְּתִתָּךְ לַנֶּפֶשׁ כֹּחַ הַדֵּעָה. אֲשֶׁר בָּהּ
תְּקוּעָה. 360

וַיְהִי הַמַּדָּע מָקוֹר כְּבוֹדָהּ.

וְעַל כֵּן לֹא יִשְׁלַט עָלֶיהָ כִּלָּיוֹן וְתִתְקַיָּם כְּפִי קִיּוּם יְסוֹדָהּ.
וְזֶה עִנְיָנָהּ וְסוֹדָהּ:

וְהַנֶּפֶשׁ הַחֲכָמָה לֹא תִרְאֶה מָוֶת. אַךְ תְּקַבֵּל עַל עֲוֹנָהּ
עֹנֶשׁ מַר מִמָּוֶת: 365

וְאִם טָהֲרָה תָּפִיק רָצוֹן. וְתִשְׂחַק לְיוֹם אַחֲרוֹן.

וְאִם נִטְמְאָה תָּנוּד בְּשֶׁצֶף קֶצֶף וְחָרוֹן:

וְכָל יְמֵי טֻמְאָתָהּ בְּבָדָד תֵּשֵׁב גּוֹלָה וְסוּרָה.

בְּכָל קֹדֶשׁ לֹא תִגָּע וְאֶל הַמִּקְדָּשׁ לֹא תָבֹא עַד מְלֹאת
יְמֵי טָהֳרָהּ: 370

49

XXXI

Who can repay your goodness?

You gave the soul to the body to give it life, teach it, and
show it the right path to keep it from evil.

You formed man from a handful of dust into which you
breathed a soul, imparting wisdom to him and
distinguishing him from the beasts.

We live on a higher plane, in a higher sphere.

You have set him in the enclosure of our world,

on which you look down from beyond

and you see him wherever he tries to hide and know what
he does,

observing always "from inside and from outside."*

XXXII

Who can penetrate the secret of your accomplishments?

You equipped the body to do your bidding,

giving it eyes to see your signs, ears to hear of your
miracles, mind to grasp some small part of your mystery,
a mouth to proclaim your praise, and a tongue to speak
of your majesty to each and all,

as I do here and now, your servant, the son of your
handmaid.

With my faint voice and my poor talent, I do what I can to
give the least hint of your greatness, a shadow of your
sublime shadow

*Exod. xxv, 11.

לא

מִי יִגְמוֹל עַל טוֹבוֹתֶיךָ בְּתִתְּךָ הַנְּשָׁמָה לַגּוּף לְהַחֲיוֹתוֹ.

וְאוֹרַח חַיִּים לְהוֹרוֹתוֹ וּלְהַרְאוֹתוֹ.

לְהַצִּיל לוֹ מֵרָעָתוֹ:

קְרַצְתּוֹ מֵאֲדָמָה. וְנָפַחְתָּ בּוֹ נְשָׁמָה.

375 וְאָצַלְתָּ עָלָיו רוּחַ חָכְמָה. אֲשֶׁר בָּהּ יִבָּדֵל מִבְּהֵמָה.

וְיַעֲלֶה אֶל מַעֲלָה רָמָה:

שַׂמְתּוֹ בְּעוֹלָמְךָ סָגוּר וְאַתָּה מִחוּץ תָּכִין מַעֲשָׂיו וְתִרְאֶנּוּ.

וְכָל אֲשֶׁר מִמְּךָ יַעֲלִימֶנּוּ. מִבַּיִת וּמִחוּץ תְּצַפֶּנּוּ:

לב

מִי יוֹדֵעַ סוֹד מִפְעֲלוֹתֶיךָ.

380 בַּעֲשׂוֹתְךָ לַגּוּף צָרְכֵי פְעֻלָּתֶיךָ.

וְנָתַתָּ לוֹ עֵינַיִם לִרְאוֹת אוֹתוֹתֶיךָ.

וְאָזְנַיִם לִשְׁמוֹעַ נוֹרְאוֹתֶיךָ.

וְרַעְיוֹן לְהָבִין קְצָת סוֹדוֹתֶיךָ.

וּפֶה לְסַפֵּר תְּהִלָּתֶךָ.

385 וְלָשׁוֹן לְהַגִּיד לְכָל יָבֹא גְּבוּרָתֶךָ.

כָּמוֹנִי הַיּוֹם אֲנִי עַבְדְּךָ בֶּן אֲמָתֶךָ.

הַמְסַפֵּר כְּפִי קֹצֶר לְשׁוֹנִי מְעַט מִזְעָר מֵרוֹמְמוֹתֶךָ.

from which the wise may perhaps infer something of your
wonders and by extrapolation try to imagine how great
they must be, for "they are life to those who find
them."*

By these marvels men can recognize you and acknowledge
that you exist, even if they cannot see your face and
your splendor.

Who has not heard of you and your power? Who then can
deny your Godhead or refuse to let your truth into his
heart?

What in this world is worth thinking of but how best to
serve you?

Therefore I take up my pen and dare the undertaking,
resolving to do my best to speak of my God

to add to his praises the faintest echo of an echo in the hope
that my iniquities may be overlooked,

for "how else could he be reconciled to his lord, except on
these heads?"**

XXXIII

O God, I am ashamed, mortified to stand before you
knowing what I know:

as great as is your glory, so is my vileness great and my
insignificance;

as mighty as you are, by that measure am I feeble; as
intelligent as you are, to that degree am I stupid.

*Prov. iv, 22.
**I Sam. xxix, 4.

וְהֵן אֵלֶּה קְצוֹת דְּרָכֶיךָ:

וּמָה עָצְמוּ רָאשֵׁיהֶם. כִּי חַיִּים הֵם לְמוֹצְאֵיהֶם

בָּהֶם יוּכְלוּ כָל שׁוֹמְעֵיהֶם לְהַכִּירֶךָ. 390

וְאִם לֹא רָאוּ פְּנֵי יְקָרֶךָ.

וְכֹל אֲשֶׁר לֹא יִשְׁמַע גְּבוּרָתֶךָ.

אֵיךְ יַכִּיר אֱלֹהוּתֶךָ.

וְאֵיךְ תָּבֹא בְלִבּוֹ אֲמִתּוּתֶךָ.

וִיכַוֵּן רַעְיוֹנָיו לַעֲבוֹדָתֶךָ: 395

עַל כֵּן מָצָא עַבְדְּךָ אֶת לִבּוֹ לִזְכּוֹר לִפְנֵי אֱלֹהָיו. מְעַט
מִזְעָר מֵרָאשֵׁי תְהִלּוֹתָיו.

אוּלַי בָם מֵעֲוֹנוֹ יַשָּׁה. וּבַמָּה יִתְרַצֶּה זֶה אֶל אֲדֹנָיו הֲלֹא
בְרָאשֵׁי:

לג

אֱלֹהַי בֹּשְׁתִּי וְנִכְלַמְתִּי לַעֲמוֹד לְפָנֶיךָ לְדַעְתִּי 400

כִּי כְפִי עָצְמַת גְּדֻלָּתְךָ כֵּן תַּכְלִית דַּלּוּתִי וְשִׁפְלוּתִי:

וּכְפִי תֹקֶף יְכָלְתְּךָ כֵּן חֻלְשַׁת יְכָלְתִּי:

וּכְפִי שְׁלֵמוּתְךָ כֵּן חֶסְרוֹן יְדִיעָתִי.

You are one, a completeness. You are life. You are
powerful and eternal, magnificent and wise. You are
God.

And I am mud, worms, dust, a bucket of guilt and shame, a
mute stone.

I am a fleeting shadow, "a wind that passes and does not
come again."*

I am the viper's venom. I am devious and crooked. I am
uncircumcised of heart.

I am hot tempered, quick to take offense, proud,
sharp-tongued, a conniver, an impostor, a knave, and a
cheat.

What am I ? What is my life? Where is that strength of
righteousness to which I once aspired?

The accounting of my days is dismal, utter ruin, a dead loss,
and when I am dead I shall be altogether forgotten.

From nothing I came and to nothing I return,

and I come before you, "not according to the law"** but
with an insolent look

*Ps. lxxviii, 39.
**Esther. iv, 16.

54

כִּי אַתָּה אֶחָד וְאַתָּה חַי וְאַתָּה גִּבּוֹר וְאַתָּה קַיָּם וְאַתָּה

405 גָּדוֹל וְאַתָּה חָכָם וְאַתָּה אֱלֹהַּ:

וַאֲנִי גּוּשׁ וְרִמָּה. עָפָר מִן הָאֲדָמָה.

כְּלִי מָלֵא כְלִמָּה. אֶבֶן דּוּמָה:

צֵל עוֹבֵר רוּחַ הוֹלֵךְ וְלֹא יָשׁוּב. חֲמַת עַכְשׁוּב:

עָקוֹב הַלֵּב. עֲרַל לֵב.

410 גְּדָל חֵמָה. חֹרֵשׁ אָוֶן וּמִרְמָה:

גְּבַהּ עֵינַיִם. קְצַר אַפַּיִם. טְמֵא שְׂפָתַיִם.

נָעֲקַשׁ דְּרָכִים. וְאָץ בְּרַגְלַיִם:

מָה אֲנִי מָה חַיַּי וּמָה גְּבוּרָתִי. וּמַה־צִּדְקָתִי.

נֶחְשָׁב לְאַיִן כָּל יְמֵי הֱיוֹתִי. וְאַף כִּי אַחֲרֵי מוֹתִי:

415 מֵאַיִן מוֹצָאִי. וּלְאַיִן מוֹבָאִי.

וְהִנֵּה בָאתִי לְפָנֶיךָ אֲשֶׁר לֹא כַדָּת בְּעַזּוּת פָּנִים. וְטֻמְאַת
רַעְיוֹנִים.

and with unclean thoughts, selfish and lewd, craving
    trinkets and baubles,
with a corrupt heart and a body plagued with foulnesses
    and disease "in a mixed multitude,"*
having gone from bad to worse, having fallen until I cannot
    fall any lower.

XXXIV

O God, I know my sins are beyond reckoning, too great,
    too gross, too mean, and too many.
But I shall confess some small part—a drop, say, of that
    ocean,
and pray that the waves that break with a roar on the rocky
    shore
may yet ebb back into silence as you "hear in heaven and
    forgive."**
    I have abrogated your commandments, I have broken
        your law,
    I have closed my heart, I have dirtied my mouth with
        slander,
    I have exercised bad judgment, I have failed those who
        trusted me,
    I have gossiped, I have harbored grudges, I have ignored
        your chastisements,
    I have joked at the wrong time, I have kept still when I
        should have spoken out,
    I have lied, I have misled people by telling partial truths,
    I have nodded in assent to wrongdoing I should have
        protested,

*Num. xi, 4.
**1 Kings viii, 34.

וְיֵצֶר זוֹנֶה. לְגִלּוּלָיו פּוֹנֶה:

וְתַאֲוָה מִתְגַּבְּרָה. וְנֶפֶשׁ לֹא מְטֹהָרָה.

וְלֵב טָמֵא. אוֹבֵד וְנִדְמָה. 420

וְגוּף נָגוּף מְלֹא אֲסַפְסוּף. יוֹסִיף וְלֹא יָסוּף:

לד

אֱלֹהַי יָדַעְתִּי כִּי עֲוֹנוֹתַי עָצְמוּ מִסַּפֵּר. וְאַשְׁמוֹתַי עָצְמוּ
מִלִּזְכּוֹר:

אַךְ אֶזְכּוֹר מֵהֶם כְּמִפָּה מִן הַיָּם. וְאֶתְוַדֶּה בָהֶם אוּלַי
אַשְׁבִּיחַ שְׁאוֹן גַּלֵּיהֶם וְדָכְיָם. 425

וְאַתָּה תִשְׁמַע הַשָּׁמַיִם וְסָלָחְתָּ:

אָשַׁמְתִּי בְתוֹרָתָךְ. בָּזִיתִי בְמִצְוֹתֶיךָ.

נָעַלְתִּי בְלִבִּי וּבְמוֹ פִי. דִּבַּרְתִּי דֹפִי.

הֶעֱוֵיתִי. וְהִרְשַׁעְתִּי. זַדְתִּי. חָמַסְתִּי. טָפַלְתִּי שָׁקֶר. יָעַצְתִּי
רַע לְאֵין חֵקֶר. 430

I have been overbearing, I have been perverse, I have
    questioned your teaching,
I have ridiculed, I have scoffed, I have turned away from
    the life you have prescribed,
I have been unfair, I have been violent, I have been
    wicked,
I have been execrable, I have yammered when I ought
    to have been patient,
and I have zigzagged when the path you had set for me
    was straight and true.
"But you are just in all that is brought upon me; for you
    have dealt fairly and I have done wickedly."*

XXXV

O God, I stare at the ground, mortified at what I have done
    to offend you.
The good you have done me, I have repaid with
    wickedness.
You created me not out of need but grace, not through any
    necessity but only out of love.
Before I existed, you showed me mercy by breathing spirit
    into me and giving me life,
and after I came forth into the light and air, you did not
    abandon me but like a fond father watched over me.

*Neh. ix, 33.

כִּזַּבְתִּי. לַצְתִּי. מָרַדְתִּי. נִאַצְתִּי. סָרַרְתִּי. עָוִיתִי. פָּשַׁעְתִּי.
צָרַרְתִּי וְעֹרֶף הִקְשֵׁיתִי.

קַצְתִּי בְתוֹכְחוֹתָיךְ רָשַׁעְתִּי.

שִׁחַתִּי דְרָכַי. תָּעִיתִי מִמַּהֲלָכַי.

עָבַרְתִּי מִמִּצְוֹתָיךְ וְסָרְתִּי. וְאַתָּה צַדִּיק עַל כָּל הַבָּא עָלַי   435
כִּי אֱמֶת עָשִׂיתָ וַאֲנִי הִרְשָׁעְתִּי:

לה

אֱלֹהַי נָפְלוּ פָנַי בְּזָכְרִי כָּל אֲשֶׁר הִכְעַסְתִּיךְ. כִּי עַל כָּל
טוֹבוֹת שֶׁגְּמַלְתַּנִי רָעָה גְמַלְתִּיךְ:

כִּי בְרָאתַנִי לֹא לְצָרְךְ רַק נְדָבָה. וְלֹא בְהַכְרֵחַ כִּי אִם
בְּרָצוֹן וְאַהֲבָה: 440

וְטֶרֶם הֱיוֹתִי בְחַסְדְּךְ קִדַּמְתָּנִי. וְנָפַחְתָּ רוּחַ בִּי וְהֶחֱיִיתָנִי.

וְאַחֲרֵי צֵאתִי לְאוֹר הָעוֹלָם לֹא עֲזַבְתָּנִי. אֲבָל כְּאָב
חוֹמֵל גִּדַּלְתָּנִי.

I was a suckling babe, and you nursed me and set me at my
  mother's breast.

You filled me with the delights of childhood and, when I
  was strong enough to stand, helped me to my feet.

You took me in your arms and taught me to walk and gave
  me wisdom and standards of righteousness.

You protected me from sorrow and trouble and, after your
  anger had passed, hid me in the shadow of your hand.

How many griefs did you keep me from seeing and from
  how much anguish did you spare me!

Before a blow came, you prepared a remedy for my
  wound, about which I knew nothing.

When I did not guard myself from danger, you guarded
  me.

When I found myself in the jaws of lions, you broke
  their teeth and delivered me to safety.

When I languished with diseases, you, out of kindness,
  healed me.

Your dreadful judgment came upon the world, but even
  then you saved me from the sword.

וְכָאמֵן אֶת הַיּוֹנֵק אֲמַנְתָּנִי . עַל שְׁדֵי אִמִּי הִבְטַחְתָּנִי

445 וּמִנְעִימוֹתָיִךְ הִשְׁבַּעְתָּנִי . וּבְבֹאִי לַעֲמוֹד עַל עָמְדִי
חִזַּקְתָּנִי .

וְקַחְתַּנִי עַל זְרֹעוֹתָיִךְ וְתִרְגַּלְתָּנִי . וְחָכְמָה וּמוּסָר לִמַּדְתָּנִי .

וּמִכָּל צָרָה וְצוּקָה חִלַּצְתָּנִי . וּבְעֵת עֲבָר זַעַם בְּצֵל יָדְךָ
הִסְתַּרְתָּנִי .

450 וְכַמָּה צָרוֹת נָעָלְמוּ מֵעֵינַי וּמֵהֶם גְּאַלְתָּנִי . וּבְטֶרֶם בָּא
הַתְּלָאָה הִקְדַּמְתָּ רְפוּאָה לְמַכָּתִי וְלֹא הוֹדַעְתָּנִי .

וּבְעֵת לֹא נִשְׁמַרְתִּי מִכָּל נֶזֶק אַתָּה שְׁמַרְתָּנִי . וּבְבֹאִי בֵּין
שְׁנֵי אֲרָיוֹת שְׁבַּרְתָּ מַלְתְּעֹת כְּפִירִים וּמִשָּׁם הוֹצֵאתָנִי .

וּבְחוּל עָלַי חֳלָיִים רָעִים וְנֶאֱמָנִים חִנָּם רְפָאתָנִי . וּבְבֹא
455 שְׁפָטֶיךָ הָרָעִים עַל הָעוֹלָם מֵחָרֶב הִצַּלְתָּנִי .

You spared me during times of pestilence and fed me in
   famine, sustaining me with plenty.
When I transgressed, you chastised me as a man chastises his
   son.
And when I called to you in sorrow, you took pity on me
   because my soul was precious to you, and you did not
   turn me away unanswered.
But more than any of this, you gave me a perfect faith to
   believe in you and know that you are the true God,
that your laws are true and your prophets speak the truth.
You did not set me among the heathen who reject you or
   among foolish people who blaspheme your name,
mock at the law, threaten your servants, and reject the
   words of your prophets.
They make a show of innocence but underneath is perfidy.
   They appear to be clean but within there is a leprous
   spot.
They are like an amphora of ordure that has been scrubbed
   bright on the outside, but "all that is in it is still
   unclean"* and noxious.

*Lev. xi, 33.

וּמִדַּבָּר מִלַּטְתָּנִי. וּבְרָעָב זַנְתָּנִי.

וּבְשָׂבָע כִּלְכַּלְתָּנִי.

וּבְהַכְעִיסִי אוֹתְךָ כַּאֲשֶׁר יְיַסֵּר אִישׁ אֶת בְּנוֹ יִסַּרְתָּנִי.

וּבְקָרְאִי מִצָּרְתִי נַפְשִׁי יָקְרָה בְּעֵינֶיךָ וְרֵיקָם לֹא הֲשִׁיבוֹתָנִי

וְעוֹד הִגְדַּלְתָּ וְהוֹסַפְתָּ עַל כָּל זֶה.　　460

בְּתִתְּךָ לִי אֱמוּנָה שְׁלֵמָה לְהַאֲמִין כִּי אַתָּה אֵל אֱמֶת.
וְתוֹרָתְךָ אֱמֶת וּנְבִיאֶיךָ אֱמֶת:

וְלֹא נָתַתָּ לִי חֵלֶק עִם מוֹרְדֶיךָ וְקָמֶיךָ. וְעַם נָבָל נִאֲצוּ
שְׁמֶךָ:

אֲשֶׁר בְּתוֹרָתְךָ יַלְעִיבוּ. וּבְעוֹבְדֶיךָ יָרִיבוּ.　　465

וּנְבִיאֶיךָ יְכַזִּיבוּ:

מַרְאִים תֻּמָּה. וְתַחְתֶּיהָ עָרְמָה:

מַרְאִים נֶפֶשׁ זַכָּה וְנִטְהָרֶת. וְתַחְתֶּיהָ תַּעֲמוֹד הַבַּהֶרֶת.

כִּכְלִי מָלֵא כְלִמָּה. רָחוּץ מִחוּץ בְּמֵי עָרְמָה.

וְכָל אֲשֶׁר בְּתוֹכוֹ יִטְמָא:　　470

XXXVI

Of all the mercies you have shown your servant, I am
    unworthy O God, and the truth you have revealed to
    me, I did not deserve.
Nevertheless, O God, I presume to praise you,
for you endowed me with a holy soul,
which, in my thoughts and actions, I have sullied, profaned,
    and defiled.
But by my sins, I never injured you but only myself.
I understood that, but a terrible tempter stands at my right
    hand, vigilant and sly.
I have good intentions but he is an adversary who never
    gives me rest or lets me catch my breath.
I have tried to haul him out of the wallow of his lusts with
    a double bridle, but my strength was not equal to his.
He balked, stood his ground, cursed, and made me curse in
    answer.
I try to think simply and clearly, but he complicates,
    qualifies, fabricates and confuses.
I propose a peace but he is implacably warlike.
He loves to humiliate me, to make me his footstool.
How often have I prepared to fight against him with
    prayers and repentance, and pious thoughts of your
    mercies ordered like troops on a battlefield.

קָטֹנְתִּי מִכֹּל הַחֲסָדִים וּמִכָּל הָאֱמֶת אֲשֶׁר עָשִׂיתָ אֶת
עַבְדֶּךָ. אָמְנָם יְיָ אֱלֹהַי אוֹדֶךָ:

כִּי נָתַתָּ בִּי נֶפֶשׁ קְדוֹשָׁה. וּבְמַעֲשַׂי הָרָעִים טִמֵּאתִיהָ.
וּבְיִצְרִי הָרַע חִלַּלְתִּיהָ וְגֵאַלְתִּיהָ:

אַךְ יָדַעְתִּי. כִּי אִם הִרְשַׁעְתִּי.   475

לֹא לְךָ רַק לְעַצְמִי הֲרֵעוֹתִי.

אֲבָל יִצְרִי הָאַכְזָר נִצָּב עַל יְמִינִי לְשִׂטְנִי.

לֹא יִתְּנֵנִי הָשֵׁב רוּחִי. וּלְהָכִין מְנוּחִי.

וְזֶה כַּמֶּה לַהֲבִיאוֹ בְכֶפֶל רִסְנֵי חָשַׁבְתִּי. וְהִתְאַרְתִּי לְהָשִׁיבוֹ

מֵי הַתַּאֲווֹת אֶל הַיַּבָּשָׁה וְלֹא יָכֹלְתִּי.   480

הֵנִיא מַחְשְׁבוֹתַי. וְחִלֵּל מוֹצָא שְׂפָתָי.

אֲנִי חוֹשֵׁב מַחְשָׁבוֹת תָּמָּה. וְהוּא חוֹרֵשׁ אָוֶן וּמִרְמָה.

אֲנִי לְשָׁלוֹם וְהוּא לְמִלְחָמָה.

עַד שָׂמֵנִי לְרַגְלָיו הֲדוֹם. וַיָּשֶׂם דְּמֵי מִלְחָמָה בְּשָׁלוֹם.

וְכַמֶּה פְעָמִים יָצָאתִי. לְהִלָּחֵם עִמּוֹ וְעָרַכְתִּי.   485

מַחֲנֵה עֲבוֹדָתִי וּתְשׁוּבָתִי. וְשַׂמְתִּי מַחֲנֵה רַחֲמֶיךָ לְעֻמָּתִי
לְעָזְרֵנִי.

I said, if the tempter "comes to the one company and
destroys it, then the company that remains will escape."*
And that was what happened,
for he scattered my forces and prevailed over me, and
nothing remained in the field but the host of your
mercies.
But they will save me. They are better than any sanctuary.
With them I may yet conquer.
"Perhaps I may be able to defeat them and drive them from
the land."**

XXXVII

May it please you, O Lord, my God to repress my lusts and
ignore my sins and transgressions.
"Do not carry me off in the middle of my days,"***
not until I have prepared for my departure, and equipped
myself for the journey.
If I leave my life as I came into it and return as naked as the
day I was born, why was I created and why have I
endured all these sorrows?
It would be better never to have been born than to
contribute to the sins of this world and its transgressions.

*Gen. xxxii, 8.
**Num. xxii, 6.
***Ps. cii, 24.

כִּי אָמַרְתִּי אִם יָבֹא יִצְרִי אֶל הַמַּחֲנָה הָאַחַת וְהִכָּהוּ וְהָיָה
הַמַּחֲנֶה הַנִּשְׁאָר לִפְלֵיטָה וְכַאֲשֶׁר חָשַׁבְתִּי כֵּן הָיָה.

490 וְהִנֵּה גָבַר עָלָי. וְהֵפִיץ חֵילָי.

וְלֹא נִשְׁאַר אֵלָי. כִּי אִם מַחֲנֵה רַחֲמֶיךָ.

אַךְ אֵדַע כִּי בָם אֲתַקְּפָנּוּ. וְיִהְיוּ לִי מֵעִיר לַעֲזוֹר אוּלַי
אוּכַל נַכֵּה בֹו וַאֲנָרְשֶׁנּוּ:

לז

יְהִי רָצוֹן מִלְּפָנֶיךָ יְיָ אֱלֹהַי לָכוֹף אֶת יִצְרִי הָאַכְזָרִי
495 וְהַסְתֵּר פָּנֶיךָ מֵחֲטָאַי וּמֵאֲשָׁמָי. אַל תַּעֲלֵנִי בַּחֲצִי יָמָי:

עַד אָכִין צָרְכִּי. לְדַרְכִּי.

וְצֵידָתִי. לְיוֹם נְסִיעָתִי.

כִּי אִם אֵצֵא מֵעוֹלָמִי כַּאֲשֶׁר בָּאתִי. וְאָשׁוּב עָרוֹם לִמְקֹמִי
כַּאֲשֶׁר יָצָאתִי.

500 לָמָּה נִבְרֵאתִי. וְלִרְאוֹת עָמָל נִקְרֵאתִי:

טוֹב לִי עוֹד אֲנִי שָׁם. מִצָּאתִי לְהַגְדִּיל פֶּשַׁע וּלְהַרְבֹּת
אָשָׁם:

O God, I pray you, judge me in mercy and "not in your anger, lest you reckon me as nothing."*

For what is man that he can bear your scrutiny? A vanity, a passing vapor! How can you weigh that in a balance?

He is like air on the scales, neither heavy nor light, nothing to weigh or measure.

From the day of his birth, he is beset and tormented, stricken, smitten by God, and afflicted.

His youth is like chaff in the wind; his old age is dry straw. In between, he is grass trodden into the earth.

He flees, but God pursues him.

From the moment he comes out of his mother's womb, his nights are grief and his days are groaning.

If today is good, tomorrow will cover him with maggots.

A grain of pollen terrifies him, and, as he flees, the thorns of bushes scratch him.

In times of prosperity, he does evil and, when he is hungry, he sins for a crust of bread.

He runs after money, forgetting that death chases behind him.

He is a smooth talker: in bad times, he promises the earth, but then, in good times, he forgets what he said and breaks all his vows.

*Jer. x, 24.

אָנָּא הָאֱלֹהִים בְּמִדַּת רַחֲמֶיךָ שְׁפָטֵנִי. אַל בְּאַפְּךָ פֶּן תַּמְעִיטֵנִי:

כִּי מָה הָאָדָם כִּי תְדִינֵהוּ. וְהָבֶל נִדָּף אֵיךְ בְּמִשְׁקָל תְּבִיאֵהוּ.

וּבַעֲלוֹתוֹ בְּמֹאזְנֵי מִשְׁפָּט לֹא יִכְבַּד וְלֹא יֵקַל. וּמַה יִּסְכָּן לְךָ לַעֲשׂוֹת לָרוּחַ מִשְׁקָל:

מִיּוֹם הֱיוֹתוֹ הוּא נִגָּשׂ וַנַעֲנֶה. נָגוּעַ מֻכֵּה אֱלֹהִים וּמְעֻנֶּה:

רֵאשִׁיתוֹ מֹץ נִהְדָּף. וְאַחֲרִיתוֹ קַשׁ נִדָּף.

וּבְחַיָּיו כְּעֵשֶׂב נִשְׁדָּף. וְהָאֱלֹהִים יְבַקֵּשׁ אֶת נִרְדָּף:

מִיּוֹם צֵאתוֹ מֵרֶחֶם אִמּוֹ. יָגוֹן לֵילוֹ וַאֲנָחָה יוֹמוֹ:

אִם הַיּוֹם יָרוּם. מָחָר תּוֹלָעִים יָרֻם:

הַמֹּץ יִדְפָנּוּ. וְהַקּוֹץ יִנְפָּנּוּ:

אִם יִשְׂבַּע יִרְשָׁע. וְאִם יִרְעַב עַל פַּת לֶחֶם יִפְשָׁע:

לִרְדוֹף הָעשֶׁר קָלּוּ אֲשׁוּרָיו. וְיִשְׁכַּח הַמָּוֶת וְהוּא אַחֲרָיו:

בְּעֵת הַמֵּצַר יָרַב אֲמָרָיו. וְיַחֲלִיק דְּבָרָיו.

69

He puts padlocks on his gates, but death is already inside
the house.

He puts watchmen on the walls, but the enemy is hiding in
his private quarters.

No fence can keep this wolf from his flock.

Man is born, not knowing why. He rejoices, not knowing
for what. And he lives, not knowing how long.

As a child, he is willful and stubborn. As a young man, he
feels lust stirring in him, and greed for wealth, and
restlessness.

He wants to board ships or venture into the desert. He will
trek into lion country, searching for glory and loot.

But the thief lies in wait for him, and suddenly he is left
with nothing.

Risk is everywhere and troubles that beset him and then
return. At every moment misery impends.

Each day is full of terrors.

וַיַּרְבָּה נְדָרָיו. וּבְצֵאתוֹ לַמֶּרְחָב יַחֵל דְּבָרָיו.

וְיִשְׁכַּח נְדָרָיו. וִיחַזֵּק בְּרִיחֵי שְׁעָרָיו.

וְהַמָּוֶת בַּחֲדָרָיו: 520

וַיַּרְבָּה שׁוֹמְרִים מִכָּל עֵבֶר. וְהָאוֹרֵב יוֹשֵׁב לוֹ בַּחָדָר.

וְהַזְּאֵב לֹא יַעֲצָרֶנּוּ גָּדֵר. מִבֹּא אֶל הָעֵדֶר:

בָּא וְלֹא יָדַע לָמָּה. וְיִשְׂמַח וְלֹא יָדַע בַּמָּה. וִיחִי וְלֹא יָדַע
כַּמָּה.

בְּיַלְדוּתוֹ. הוֹלֵךְ בִּשְׁרִירוּתוֹ. 525

וְכַאֲשֶׁר תָּחֵל רוּחַ הַתַּאֲוָה לְפַעֲמוֹ. יִתְעוֹרֵר לֶאֱסוֹף חַיִל
נָהוֹן וְיִסַּע מִמְּקוֹמוֹ.

לִרְכּוֹב אֳנִיּוֹת. וְלִרְדּוֹף בַּצִּיּוֹת.

וּלְהָבִיא נַפְשׁוֹ בִּמְעוֹנוֹת אֲרָיוֹת. וְהִיא מִתְהַלָּכֶת בֵּין
הַחַיּוֹת: 530

וּבְחָשְׁבוֹ כִּי רַב הוֹדוֹ. וְכִי כַבִּיר מָצְאָה יָדוֹ.

בַּשָּׁלוֹם שׁוֹדֵד יְבוֹאֵנּוּ. וְעֵינָיו פָּקַח וְאֵינֶנּוּ:

בְּכָל עֵת הוּא מְזֻמָּן לַתְּלָאוֹת. חוֹלְפוֹת וּבָאוֹת.

וּבְכָל שָׁעוֹת לִמְאֹרָעוֹת:

71

Should he find a brief respite, it will cost him: disasters will swarm and afflictions will gather about him.

War will break out: a sword will cut him, or an arrowhead pierce his body.

Calamities will surround him in a flood, drowning him. Evil will find him out.

He will be a burden to himself and hate his life. The honey on his table will taste like the venom of serpents.

His body will ache, and his honor will be destroyed.

Urchins will laugh at him, and children and fools have authority over him.

His friends will desert him and deny that they know him.

His time will come, and he will leave the rooms of his house to wait in the foyer of Death.

From the cozy dark of his bedroom, he will be ushered into the gloom of Death's waiting room.

There, they will take his rich brocade and his fancy purple garments, and give him a shroud, wormy and moth-eaten.

He will lie down in the dust and return to the dust he was made of.

This is man's fate. When does he have time to repent, to wash away the filth of sin and vileness?

The time is short and the task is huge.*

---

*cf. *Ethics of the Fathers*, ii, 20. Rabbi Tarphon said, "The day is short, the work is great, the workers are lazy, the reward is much, and the master of the house presses."

בְּכָל הָרְגָעִים. לְפָנָעִים.

וּבְכָל הַיָּמִים. עָלָיו אֵימִים:

אִם רֶגַע יַעֲמֹד בְּשַׁלְוָה. פֶּתַע תְּבוֹאֵהוּ הֹוָה:

אוֹ בְמִלְחָמָה יָבֹא וְחָרֶב תְּנַפְּצֵהוּ. אוֹ קֶשֶׁת נְחוּשָׁה תַּחְלְפֵהוּ

אוֹ יַקִּיפוּהוּ יְגוֹנִים. יִשְׁטְפוּהוּ מַיִם זֵידוֹנִים.

אוֹ יִמְצָאוּהוּ חֳלָיִים רָעִים וְנֶאֱמָנִים:

עַד יִהְיֶה לְמַשָּׂא עַל נַפְשׁוֹ. וְיִמְצָא מְרוֹרַת פְּתָנִים בְּדִבְשׁוֹ:

וּבְעֵת כְּאֵבוֹ יִגְדַּל. כְּבוֹדוֹ יִדַּל:

וּנְעָרִים יִתְקַלְּסוּ בוֹ. וְתַעֲלוּלִים יִמְשְׁלוּ בוֹ:

וְיִהְיֶה לְטֹרַח עַל יוֹצְאֵי מֵעָיו. וְיִתְנַכְּרוּ לוֹ כָּל רֵעָיו:

וּבְבֹא עִתּוֹ יֵצֵא מֵחֲצָרָיו לַחֲצַר מָוֶת. וּמִצֵּל חֲדָרָיו לְצַלְמָוֶת:

וְיִפְשַׁט רִקְמָה וְתוֹלָע. וְיִלְבַּשׁ רִמָּה וְתוֹלָע:

וְלֶעָפָר יִשְׁכָּב. וְיָשׁוּב אֶל יְסוֹדוֹ אֲשֶׁר מִמֶּנּוּ חֻצָּב:

וְאִישׁ אֲשֶׁר אֵלֶּה לוֹ מָתַי יִמְצָא עֵת תְּשׁוּבָה. לִרְחֹץ חֶלְאַת מְשׁוּבָה.

וְהַיּוֹם קָצַר וְהַמְּלָאכָה מְרֻבָּה:

The bosses are impatient and Time laughs at him.
The proprietor fumes and wants results.
O God, remember these troubles that come to men:
if I have done wickedness, be good to me in my old age.
Do not give measure for measure, for man would then be
hopeless, his sins being measureless,
and we should all die in despair "and with no one's
regret."*

XXXVIII

O God, my sins are too heavy to bear,
but for your name's sake, what will you do for me?
If I cannot hope for your mercies, to whom else can I look
for pity?
You can kill me, but still my hope will be in you.
If you harry me because of my wickedness, I will flee from
you, and find my hiding place in you.
In your own shadow will I find shelter from your anger.
To the skirts of your mercy will I cling until you relent and
bless me.
You made me from clay, from dirt, and then you tested me
with a battering of griefs.
Do not blame me for my imperfections nor feed me the
bitter fruit of my deeds

*2 Chron. xxi, 20.

וְהַנּוֹגְשִׂים אָצִים. חָשִׁים וְרָצִים.

וְהַזְּמָן מִמֶּנּוּ שׂוֹחֵק. וּבַעַל הַבַּיִת דּוֹחֵק:

555 לָכֵן נָא אֱלֹהַי זְכוֹר אֵלֶּה הַתְּלָאוֹת. אֲשֶׁר עַל אָדָם
בָּאוֹת:

וְאִם אֲנִי הֲרֵעוֹתִי. אַתָּה תֵּיטִיב אַחֲרִיתִי.

וְאַל תִּגְמוֹל מִדָּה בְּמִדָּה. לְאִישׁ אֲשֶׁר עֲוֹנוֹתָיו בְּלִי מִדָּה.
וּבְמוֹתוֹ יֵלֵךְ בְּלִי חֶמְדָּה:

לח

560 אֱלֹהַי אִם עֲוֹנִי מִנְּשׂוֹא נָדוֹל. מַה תַּעֲשֶׂה לְשִׁמְךָ הַגָּדוֹל.

וְאִם לֹא אוֹחִיל לְרַחֲמֶיךָ. מִי יָחוּס עָלַי חוּץ מִמֶּךָ:

לָכֵן אִם תִּקְטְלֵנִי לְךָ אֲיַחֵל.

וְאִם תְּבַקֵּשׁ לַעֲוֹנִי אָבְרַח מִמְּךָ אֵלֶיךָ. וְאֶתְכַּסֶּה מֵחֲמָתְךָ
בְּצִלָּךְ:

565 וּבְשׁוּלֵי רַחֲמֶיךָ אַחֲזִיק עַד אִם רִחַמְתָּנִי. וְלֹא אֲשַׁלַּחֲךָ
כִּי אִם בֵּרַכְתָּנִי:

זְכָר נָא כִּי כַחֹמֶר עֲשִׂיתָנִי. וּבְאֵלֶּה הַתְּלָאוֹת נִסִּיתָנִי:

עַל כֵּן לֹא תִפְקוֹד עָלַי בְּמַעֲלָלָי. וְאַל תַּאֲכִילֵנִי פְּרִי
פְעָלָי.

but forbear, be patient, and do not hurry me to my last days
until I have prepared.

Do not hustle me from the earth with my arms still filthy
from the mixing-bowl of my sins.

When you put my sins in the balance, put my sorrows on
the other side of the scale.

If you think of my wickedness and insolence, think also of
my heartaches and figure them into my account.

Remember me, O God, and consider my life of exile. I
have wandered the earth like Cain,

and you have tempered me in the diaspora's forge.

Does this not purify some of my baseness or cleanse me of
some of my many impurities?

I believe it was for my good that you tested me, and I have
faced my afflictions as one of the faithful, trusting that, in
the end, they would count in my favor.

I believe you have brought me through my ordeals and my
miseries.

Show me your mercy, then, and do not vent your anger
upon me.

Do not punish me for my mistakes and my sins but tell
your destroying angel, "Enough"!

וְהַאֲרָךְ לִי אַפְּךָ וְאַל תַּקְרִיב יוֹמִי. עַד אָכִין צֵדָה לָשׁוּב
אֶל מְקוֹמִי:

וְאַל תֶּחֱזַק עָלַי לְמַהֵר לְשַׁלְּחַנִי מִן הָאָרֶץ וּמִשְׁאֵרוֹת
אֲשָׁמַי צְרוּרוֹת עַל שִׁכְמִי:

וּבְהַעֲלֹתְךָ בְמִשְׁקָל עֲוֹנוֹתַי. שִׂים לְךָ בְּכַף שְׁנָיָה תְּלָאוֹתַי.

וּבְזָכְרְךָ רִשְׁעִי וּמָרְדִּי. זְכָר עָנְיִי וּמְרוּדִי.

וְשִׂים אֵלֶּה נֹכַח אֵלֶּה:

וּזְכָר נָא אֱלֹהַי כִּי זֶה כַּמֶּה לָאָרֶץ נוֹד צְנַפְתָּנִי. וּבְכוֹר
נָלוּת בְּחַנְתָּנִי.

וּמֵרוֹב רִשְׁעִי צְרַפְתָּנִי. וְיָדַעְתִּי כִּי לְטוֹבָתִי נִסִּיתָנִי.

וֶאֱמוּנָה עִנִּיתָנִי.

וּלְהֵטִיב לִי בְאַחֲרִיתִי בְּמִבְחַן הַתְּלָאוֹת הֲבֵאתָנִי:

לָכֵן אֱלֹהַי יֶהֱמוּ עָלַי רַחֲמֶיךָ. וְאַל תְּכַלֶּה עָלַי זַעְמְךָ
וְאַל תִּגְמְלֵנִי כְּמַעְבָּדִי. וְאָמַר לַמַּלְאָךְ הַמַּשְׁחִית דָּי:

570
575
580

Where is my preferment now, where are my honors and
   awards of merit?
If you search out my sins, I am nothing. I am game to hunt,
   quarry with beaters out in the brush, an antelope trapped
   in a net.
My days are mostly done, and for the time left me the
   prospects are not good.
I am here today, but tomorrow, if you look for me, I shall
   be gone.
And if I die now, what was the point? What was the
   purpose? I am fuel for the great fire.
God, look upon me with kindness, favor my last days, show
   mercy to me in the time I have left.
After the hailstorm, do not let what remains of the crop be
   eaten by locusts.
I am your creature, your handiwork.
Why would you want worms to devour me, "to eat the
   fruit of the labor of your hands"?*

XXXIX

May it please you, O God, to come back to me with mercy
   or bring me back in contrition to you.
Open my heart and open your ear to my plea.
Strengthen me with your law and put the fear of you in my
   mind.

*Ps. cxxviii, 2.

וּמַה מַּעֲלָתִי וְיִתְרוֹנִי. כִּי תְבַקֵּשׁ לַעֲוֹנִי:

וְתָשִׂים עָלַי מִשְׁמָר. וּתְצָדֵנִי כָּתוֹא מִכְמָר:

הֲלֹא יָמַי חָלַף רֻבָּם וְאֵינָם. וְהַנִּשְׁאָרִים יָמַקּוּ בַּעֲוֹנָם:

וְאִם הַיּוֹם לְפָנֶיךָ הִנֵּנִי. מָחָר עֵינֶיךָ בִּי וְאֵינֶנִּי:

וְעַתָּה לָמָה אָמוּת. כִּי תֹאכְלֵנִי הָאֵשׁ הַגְּדוֹלָה הַזֹּאת:

אֱלֹהַי שִׂים עֵינֶיךָ עָלַי לְטוֹבָה לִשְׁאֵרִית יְמֵי הַמְעַטִּים.
וְאַל תִּרְדּוֹף הַשְּׂרִידִים וְהַפְּלַטִּים:

וְהַפְּלֵטָה הַנִּשְׁאֶרֶת מִבְּרַד מְהוּמוֹתַי. אַל יַחְסְלֶנָּה יָלָק
אַשְׁמוֹתָי:

כִּי יְצִיר כַּפֶּיךָ אָנִי.

וּמַה יִּסְכָּן לָךְ כִּי רָמָה תִקָּחֵנִי לָאֱכֹל. יְגִיעַ כַּפֶּיךָ **כִּי**
תֹאכַל:

לט

יְהִי רָצוֹן מִלְפָנֶיךָ יְיָ אֱלֹהַי לָשׁוּב עָלַי בְּרַחֲמֶיךָ.
וְלַהֲשִׁיבֵנִי בִּתְשׁוּבָה שְׁלֵמָה לְפָנֶיךָ.

וְלִתְחִנָּתִי תָּכִין לִבִּי תַקְשִׁיב אָזְנֶךָ. וְתִפְתַּח לִבִּי בְּתוֹרָתֶךָ.

וְתִטַּע בְּרַעְיוֹנַי יִרְאָתֶךָ:

Give me a favorable verdict and abrogate the outstanding
   writs against me.
Protect me from temptation and do not allow me to fall
   into shame, guard me from contempt, and keep me from
   occasions of evil "until these calamities are past."*
Be at my lips and my tongue lest I sin in my speech.
Remember me and remember your people who look to the
   rebuilding of the Temple.
Protect our tribes whom you have chosen and make me
   worthy to enter the sanctuary.
It is desolate now and in ruins,** but we cherish its broken
   stones and its dust.
Look at its poor rubble and rebuild.

XL

O God, I implore you. Those who beseech you have their
   good deeds to intercede for them.
They have acts of righteousness as advocates.
But in me there are no good deeds. I am barren as a
   stripped vine.
I have no virtue, no rectitude, no piety, no honor,
no prayer, no hope, no innocence, and no decency.

*Ps. lvii, 1.
**Isa. lxi, 4.

וְתִגְזֹור עָלַי גְּזֵרוֹת טוֹבוֹת. וּתְבַטֵּל מֵעָלַי גְּזֵרוֹת רָעוֹת: 600

וְאַל תְּבִיאֵנִי לִידֵי נִסָּיוֹן. וְלֹא לִידֵי בִזָּיוֹן:

וּמִכָּל פְּגָעִים רָעִים הַצִּילֵנִי. וְעַד יַעֲבוֹר הַוּוֹת בְּצִלְּךָ
תַּסְתִּירֵנִי:

וְהָיָה עִם פִּי וְהֶגְיוֹנִי. וּשְׁמוֹר דְּרָכַי מֵחֲטוֹא בִלְשׁוֹנִי:

זָכְרֵנִי בְּזִכְרוֹן וּרְצוֹן עַמֶּךָ. וּבְבִנְיַן אוּלַמֶּךָ. 605

לִרְאוֹת בְּטוֹבַת בְּחִירֶיךָ. וְחַכֵּנִי לְשַׁחַר דְּבִירֶךָ.

הַשָּׁמֵם וְהֶחָרֵב. וְלִרְצוֹת אֲבָנָיו וַעֲפָרוֹתָיו.

וְרִגְבֵי חָרְבוֹתָיו. וְתִבְנֶה שׁוֹמְמוֹתָיו:

מ

אֱלֹהַי יָדַעְתִּי כִּי הַמִּתְחַנְּנִים לְפָנֶיךָ.

יָלִיצוּ עֲלֵיהֶם מַעֲשִׂים טוֹבִים אֲשֶׁר הִקְדִּימוּ. אוֹ 610
צִדְקוֹתֵיהֶם אֲשֶׁר הֵרִימוּ.

וַאֲנִי אֵין בִּי מַעֲשִׂים כִּי אֲנִי נָעוּר וָרֵק. כְּנִפָּן בּוֹקֵק.

וְאֵין בִּי לֹא צֶדֶק וְלֹא כֹשֶׁר. לֹא חֶסֶד וְלֹא יֹשֶׁר.

לֹא תְפִלָּה וְלֹא תְחִנָּה. לֹא תָמָּה וְלֹא אֱמוּנָה.

I have no justice, no aspect of goodness.

I have not served God, I have not avoided sin.

But may it be your will, O Lord our God and God of our fathers and the sovereign of worlds, to have mercy on me and draw near to me.

Visit me with your will, bear me up to the light of your countenance, and show me your grace.

Do not reckon my worth by my deeds and make me the laughingstock of the unbelievers.

Do not take me off in the middle of my days. Do not turn away from me but purify me of my sins.

Do not cast me out of your presence, but revive me, fill me with glory, and receive me in honor and peace in the life of the hereafter.

Elevate me and let me live in glory among your saints.

Count me among those who are saved and have eternal life.

Make me worthy to shine and reflect the light of your face.

Raise me up from the depths of the earth to the heights of heaven,

לֹא צֶדֶק וְלֹא מִדָּה טוֹבָה. לֹא עֲבוֹדָה וְלֹא תְשׁוּבָה: 615

וּבְכֵן יְהִי רָצוֹן מִלְּפָנֶיךָ יְיָ אֱלֹהֵינוּ וֵאלֹהֵי אֲבוֹתֵינוּ רִבּוֹן
כָּל הָעוֹלָמִים לְרַחֵם עָלַי. וְהָיִיתָ קָרוֹב אֵלָי.

לְפָקְדֵנִי בִּפְקֻדַּת רְצוֹנֶךָ. וְלָשֵׂאת אֵלַי אוֹר פָּנֶיךָ.

וּלְהַמְצִיאֵנִי חִנָּךְ.

וּכְפִי מַעֲשַׂי אַל תִּגְמְלֵנִי. וְחֶרְפַּת נָבָל אַל תְּשִׂימֵנִי. 620

וּבַחֲצִי יָמַי אַל תַּעֲלֵנִי. וְאַל תַּסְתֵּר פָּנֶיךָ מִמֶּנִּי.

וּמַחֲטָאתִי טַהֲרֵנִי. וּמִלְּפָנֶיךָ אַל תַּשְׁלִיכֵנִי.

וּבְכָבוֹד תְּחַיֵּינִי. וְאַחַר כָּבוֹד תִּקָּחֵנִי.

וּבְעֵת מִן הָעוֹלָם הַזֶּה תּוֹצִיאֵנִי. לְחַיֵּי הָעוֹלָם הַבָּא
בְּשָׁלוֹם תְּבִיאֵנִי. 625

וְאַל עַל תִּקְרָאֵנִי. וּבֵין הַחֲסִידִים תּוֹשִׁיבֵנִי.

וְעִם הַמְּנוּיִים בְּחָלָד חֶלְקָם חַלְּקָם בַּחַיִּים תִּמְנֵנִי. וְלָאוֹר בְּאוֹר
פָּנֶיךָ תְּזַכֵּנִי.

וְתָשׁוּב תְּחַיֵּינִי. וּמִתְּהוֹמוֹת הָאָרֶץ תָּשׁוּב וְתַעֲלֵנִי.

and I shall say, "I praise you, Lord, for though you were angry with me, you softened your anger and comforted me."*

Yours is the mercy, O God, in every good thing that has happened to me and every good thing that will happen to me until the day I die,

and for this I thank you, for this I magnify and sanctify and exalt and honor you.

Allow the mouth of your creature to sing your praise.

From those who bless you, accept your own blessings on yourself.

Through those who proclaim your unity, proclaim it yourself.

With the lips of your worshipers, sing your own glory, and receive the exaltation of those you made to exalt you.

Be wafted aloft on the breath of our prayers,

for there is no god, O God, like you, and none whose works can compare with yours.

May the words of my mouth and the meditation of my heart be acceptable in your sight, O God, my strength and my redeemer.**

*Isa. xii, 1.
**Ps. xix, 14.

84

וְאֹמַר אוֹדְךָ יְיָ כִּי אָנַפְתָּ בִּי יָשֹׁב אַפְּךָ וּתְנַחֲמֵנִי. וּלְךָ יְיָ
חָסֶד עַל כָּל הַטּוֹבָה אֲשֶׁר גְּמַלְתָּנִי.

וַאֲשֶׁר עַד יוֹם מוֹתִי תִּגְמְלֵנִי.

וְעַל כָּל זֶה אֲנִי חַיָּב לְהוֹדוֹת לְהַלֵּל לְפָאֵר וּלְרוֹמֵם
אוֹתָךְ.

תִּשְׁתַּבַּח בְּפִי בְרוּאֶיךָ. תִּתְקַדֵּשׁ בְּפִי מַקְדִּישֶׁיךָ.

תִּתְיַחַד בְּפִי מְיַחֲדֶיךָ. תִּתְפָּאַר בְּפִי מְפָאֲרֶיךָ.

תִּתְרוֹמֵם בְּפִי מְרוֹמְמֶךָ. תִּתְנַשֵּׂא בְּפִי מְנַשְּׂאֶיךָ.

כִּי אֵין כָּמוֹךָ בָאֱלֹהִים אֲדֹנָי וְאֵין כְּמַעֲשֶׂיךָ:

יִהְיוּ לְרָצוֹן אִמְרֵי פִי וְהֶגְיוֹן לִבִּי לְפָנֶיךָ יְיָ צוּרִי וְגֹאֲלִי:

SELECTED
BIBLIOGRAPHY

Berlin, Adele. *Biblical Poetry Through Medieval Jewish Eyes.* Bloomington: Indiana University Press, 1991.

Biale, David. *Gershom Scholem: Kabbalah and Counter-History.* Cambridge, Mass: Harvard University.

Dan, Joseph. *Gershom Scholem and the Mystical Dimension of Jewish History.* New York: New York University Press, 1987.

Davidson, Israel, ed. *Selected Religious Poems of Solomon ibn Gabirol,* Israel Zangwill, trans. Philadelphia: Jewish Publication Society, 1923.

Frye, Northrop. *Anatomy of Criticism.* New Jersey: Princeton University Press, 1957.

Frye, Northrop. *Words With Power: Being a Second Study of the Bible and Literature.* New York: Harcourt Brace Jovanovich, 1990.

Goodman, Lenn E., ed. *Neoplatonism and Jewish Thought.* Albany: State University of New York Press, 1992.

Heinemann, Isaak. "Scientific Allegorization During the Jewish Middle Ages." In *Studies in Jewish Thought: An Anthology of*

German Jewish Scholarship, Alfred Jospe, ed. Detroit, Mich.: Wayne State University Press, 1981.

Kugel, James L., ed. *Poetry and Prophecy: The Beginnings of a Literary Tradition.* Ithaca, N.Y.: Cornell University Press, 1990.

Loewe, Raphael J. "Ibn Gabirol's Treatment of Sources in the Kether Malkuth." In *Studies in Jewish Religious and Intellectual History Presented to Alexander Altmann on the Occasion of his Seventieth Birthday*, Raphael Loewe and Siegfried Stein, eds. University: University of Alabama Press, 1979.

Loewe, Raphael J. "The Bible in Medieval Hebrew Poetry." In *Interpreting the Hebrew Bible: Essays in Honor of E. I. J. Rosenthal*, J. A. Emerton, Stefan C. Reif, eds. New York: Cambridge University Press, 1982.

Loewe, Raphael J. *Ibn Gabirol.* London: Weidenfeld and Nicolson, 1989.

Pagis, Dan. *Hebrew Poetry of the Middle Ages and the Renaissance.* Berkeley: University of California Press, 1991.

Scheindlin, Raymond P. *The Gazelle: Medieval Hebrew Poems on God, Israel, and the Soul.* Philadelphia: Jewish Publication Society, 1991.

Scholem, Gershom. *Major Trends in Jewish Mysticism.* New York: Schocken Books, 1946.

Scholem, Gershom. *Origins of the Kabbalah*, A. Arkush trans.; R. J. Zwi Werblosky ed. New Jersey: Princeton University Press, 1962.

Sendor, Mark Brian. *The Emergence of Provencal Kabbalah: Rabbi Isaac the Blind's Commentary on Sefer Yezirah.* Ann Arbor, Michigan: UMI Dissertation Services, 1994.

Smalley, Beryl. *The Study of the Bible in the Middle Ages.* Indiana: Notre Dame University Press, 1964.

Talmage, Frank. "Apples of Gold: The Inner Meaning of Sacred Texts in Medieval Judaism." In *Jewish Spirituality*, Arthur Green, ed. New York: Crossroad Publishing Company, 1986.

Tanakh: A New Translation of the Holy Scriptures. Philadelphia: Jewish Publication Society, 1985.

REED COLLEGE BOOKSTORE
3203 S.E. WOODSTOCK BLVD
PORTLAND, OR 97202
PH: 503-777-7287 FAX: 503-777-7768
EMAIL: BOOKSTORE@REED.EDU

CCOUNT SALE   001 001   0034948
ASHIER: JESSICA   11/16/98 12:41

1 GABRIOL/CROWN FOR THE KIN
    290 10134887   1 N   19.95
2 KATZ, YACOV/DIVINE LAW IN
    290 10128848   1 N   45.00
ax Exempt: 930386908

               Subtotal   64.95

    Items   2   Total   64.95

/R CHARGE   64.95
ust: DEAN'S DEVELOPMENT FUND
cct: DEPARTMENTAL
Bal: -64.95

            Change Due   0.00

       THANK YOU FOR SHOPPING AT
        REED COLLEGE BOOKSTORE